T0162174

ESCAPE PLANS

Invisible Publishing
Halifax & Toronto

ESCAPE PLANS

TERI VLASSOPOULOS

Invisible Publishing
Halifax & Toronto

Library and Archives Canada Cataloguing in Publication

Vlassopoulos, Teri, 1979-, author
    Escape plans / Teri Vlassopoulos.

Issued in print and electronic formats.
ISBN 978-1-926743-56-1 (paperback).--ISBN 978-1-926743-62-2 (epub)

    I. Title.

PS8643.L38E83 2015   C813'.6   C2015-905225-4
                                         C2015-905226-2

Cover & Interior designed by Megan Fildes

Typeset in Laurentian and Slate by Megan Fildes
With thanks to type designer Rod McDonald

Printed and bound in Canada

Invisible Publishing | Halifax & Toronto
www.invisiblepublishing.com

We acknowledge the support of the Canada Council for the Arts, which last year
invested $157 million to bring the arts to Canadians throughout the country.

Invisible Publishing recognizes the support of the Province of Nova Scotia
through the Department of Communities, Culture & Heritage. We are pleased
to work in partnership with the Culture Division to develop and promote our
cultural resources for all Nova Scotians.

For Andrew and Clara

I'm not speaking to you about things past, I'm speaking
  about love;
adorn your hair with the sun's thorns,
dark girl;
the heart of the Scorpion has set,
the tyrant in man has fled,
and all the daughters of the sea, Nereids, Graeae,
hurry toward the shimmering of the rising goddess;
whoever has never loved will love,
in the light...

— George Seferis, from *Thrush*

PROLOGUE: ZOE

My father drowned in the Aegean Sea, fifty nautical miles northeast of the port of Piraeus. When it happened, my mother and I were at home in Toronto. It was early evening in Greece, afternoon for us, and I was at school when she found out. She didn't tell me right away. After class I went to a swim practice and then I walked home and made myself a grilled cheese sandwich. The phone kept ringing and I saw my mother only in passing, but I was always pleasantly weary after swimming and associated the lingering smell of chlorine and shampoo with a kind of deep, sweet exhaustion, so I ignored the phone calls and fell asleep without saying goodnight.

My mother, in those few hours after she found out there'd been an accident, hoped that a sailor in a passing ship would find my father and pull him on-board. At the very least, she thought he could've been clinging to a piece of driftwood or a mermaid—anything—treading water and waiting patiently to be rescued. Her hope finally waned, and at dawn she woke me up. I was still lying in bed when she knelt down and rested her head on the mattress, close to mine. I sat up, bleary-eyed, and looked around my room: yellow-grey morning light filtering through the curtains, my mother on her knees, my bathing suit a damp lump on the floor where I'd discarded it the night before.

Sometimes I wonder about those few hours, how it was

possible that I could've lived through them without sensing any overarching and fundamental change. Didn't I notice a strong, cold breeze on my walk home? Did I bite my tongue or even feel ringing in my ears? I can't remember anything out of the ordinary. I mean, I was thirteen years old when it happened; it didn't occur to me to pay attention to cosmic signs.

I imagined that my father's ghost must have flown through our house, waved its hands in my face and tried to tell me something was wrong. He was a big man—his ghost would've had a heft to it. The electromagnetic forces must have been off the charts, and I didn't even notice or figure it out on my own. I want to say that I've gotten better at reading signs as I've gotten older, that I've taught myself how to become better attuned to the universe, and while I think I've improved, sometimes I'm as clueless as I was back then.

I've been to Greece twice in my life, once when I was six years old and then again for my father's funeral, so my memories of the country are either fuzzy with age or intensely, painfully bright. From my first visit, I remember my father and I walking down a steep street and riding a trolley bus. I met my grandparents too, but I remember even less about them—the musty smell of my grandmother's dresses, my grandfather's scratchy kisses. I have pictures of them holding me up like a prize fish, the two of them smiling wide, proud and triumphant. We returned to Toronto and they died before I had the chance to meet them again.

Before we left for my father's funeral, my mother told me that in his will (he had a will?), he'd requested that his body (body?) be buried in his family's tomb (tomb?) in Athens. She asked me, gently, if I minded. I was a kid and my father had just died and I don't know if she truly thought I was capable of giving her a rational answer, no matter how carefully she asked. I didn't say what I was thinking, which was that I was worried that it would be lonely for him in Greece, that there would be no one around to visit. I didn't ask her if having a family tomb meant I'd have to be buried there, too. I wondered what it meant to be buried, if it mattered where you were, ultimately. When I told Mom that it was okay, it was for her sake and not mine. It was the answer she wanted to hear and besides, the decision had already been made, so there was no use making it more complicated.

I don't know if I'll visit Greece again. I don't think my mother wants to return and the thought of going on my own, without someone to guide me or translate the language, is intimidating. My father never taught me Greek. Mom didn't speak it and when I was younger he didn't see any point in me learning; it wasn't necessary in Canada. It seeped in small increments anyway. I'd listen to my father when he called my grandparents and became accustomed to the lilt of the language. Soon after he died I wanted to learn it, though, as if it might bring me closer to him. I sat down with a book called *Learn Greek in Three Months*, and fell behind when it took me too long to memorize the alphabet. For hours I would sit and practice writing out the letters, learning the new symbols.

In Greek, there are two letters that make the *o* sound. There's omicron, which looks like the Roman alphabet *o*, and there's omega, which, in lower case, looks like a little rounded *w*. Usually the omega will come at the end of the word, while the omicron will be the *o* buried in the middle, but this isn't a hard and fast rule. In my name, Zoe, the *o* in the middle is omega, not omicron. Ζωη. I remember being satisfied that my short name had two alphabet endings: the Roman zed and Greek omega.

A few times after my father died, I would walk into a room and find my mother crying. The first time I caught her was in the kitchen over breakfast, and I had no idea what to say, so I didn't say anything.

"Zoe," she said, "do you know that your name means 'life'?" I shook my head. "Your father picked it. Your grandmother was so mad when he didn't name you after her. He'd promised he was going to."

"I didn't know that," I said.

But I did. My father loved this story, and would tell it to me often. Normally I'd cut him off, bored by my familiarity with the anecdote, but this time, my mother telling me the story and looking so sad, I pretended I didn't know, that it was the first time I'd ever heard it.

Maybe it isn't hard to keep important information from the people you love. You just meet at a comfortable halfway point of truth and semi-truth. Maybe it's better to know less than it is to know more, or to at least act like it.

I'm still trying to figure it out.

NIKO

I've always been good at leaving. I left Athens when I was twenty-three and while the lead-up had been difficult—studying, worrying about money, mandatory army service—by the time it came to leave, I was ready. I showed up at the airport four hours early and while waiting I realized that I was no longer seized with panic about my future. Jacqueline Kennedy had recently married Aristotle Onassis, and my mother thought it was a good omen, as if the union of a Greek shipping magnate and a beloved American president's widow had a bearing on my life abroad. I dismissed it at first, but when I landed in the United States, the first newspaper article I saw was about them, and for once I thought my mother was right: it was a good sign.

After that first departure, each subsequent move was easier. I assumed this momentum would carry forward to my latest decision to return to Athens from Toronto to work for Calypso, the shipping company that had once, long ago, belonged to my family, even if circumstances were different from when I'd been in my twenties.

My cousin George met me at the airport. He'd insisted on picking me up, and after saying goodbye to Anna and Zoe and then sitting through my flight in silence, I was happy to see him.

"Are you excited to see your new home?" he asked in the car as we drove into Athens.

"You tell me."

When I'd finalized my plans to take the job at Calypso, I'd asked George to help me find a place to live. I'd given him the bare minimum of criteria and within a week he'd found me something in the neighbourhood of Kypseli.

"There it is!"

He pointed to a nondescript beige building that looked similar to the nondescript beige buildings beside it. The street was lined with cars parked bumper to bumper all the way down the length of it, a few creeping up on the sidewalk. He circled the block looking for a parking spot, gave up, and then just idled by the front door while a lineup of cars developed behind us.

"Go and see the apartment on your own first," he said, and passed the keys to me. "I'll join you when I find a parking spot. If you hate it, you can think of a nice way to tell me."

The driver behind us leaned on his horn as I struggled with my suitcases, so I took my time with my last one to piss him off even more. George screeched off. I stood at the front door, put the key in the lock, but no matter how much I jiggled, it wouldn't open. An older woman came up behind me with bags of groceries while I tried a different, useless key.

"Excuse me," I said. "Do you live here?"

"Of course. Do you?"

"As of today."

"You just arrived?"

"I'm moving in on the fourth floor."

"Oh," she said, eyeing me up and down. "I've heard about you. I'm Maria." She and her husband, Spiro, lived next door to me. She let me in.

During the few weeks between George picking up the keys to the apartment and my arrival, the lock on the front door had been changed. I later found out it was changed often, due to an ongoing feud between the bakery next door and the man who lived on the first floor of my building, Yianni. He was seventy years old, but looked as though he'd been eighty-five for the last fifteen years and would continue to look as such until he died, probably at the age of one hundred. He was wrinkled and rickety and couldn't walk around the block, but after years of practice, he knew how to raise hell. His hard-headedness was persistent.

Because of a shoddy wiring job, the bakery and our adjoined apartment building shared an electrical breaker box. It was in our lobby, and occasionally the married couple who owned the bakery had to use it. Elly and Thomas were Albanian, and Yianni didn't approve of them having access to the building. After all, Albanians were prone to theft, and even if Elly and Thomas were good people, he said, their friends were a problem. Others in the building quietly agreed, but Yianni was the only one who went out of his way to shut Elly and Thomas out. Most of the time he'd just grumble about it, about how when he was younger he'd never had these problems, that it was only in the past few years with the influx of Albanian immigrants into Greece that he'd had to worry. Then he'd read an article in the newspaper about a crime supposedly perpetrated by an Albanian and would be motivated enough to use his own pension money to change the locks without consulting anyone first. One by one, each apartment would get new keys and then someone would sneak a copy to the bakery as well, and the cycle would repeat. I suspected it was Maria who slipped Elly and Thomas the keys.

The elevator was too small to fit Maria and me, my suitcases and her groceries, so I let her go up first. The key to my apartment worked fine. My landlord was a Greek man who now lived in Chicago and had kept the apartment in case he needed it in the future. He'd furnished the place sparsely, and it was small, but functional: one bedroom, a kitchen, a balcony, a desk in the front room, a couch. A silver-plated icon of Mary holding baby Jesus hung above the bed in the bedroom, but otherwise the walls were empty.

George buzzed and I let him in. "What do you think?"

"It's perfect."

He walked around the small space and explained its quirks. "You turn the hot water heater on here, and the window by the balcony sticks, so don't use it."

"I'll fix it," I said, and he laughed as if to say *Don't bother*. When he finished his tour, he handed me a small cardboard box he'd carried in with him. "This is from Katerina. She would be happy if you came over for dinner tonight."

George, his wife, Katerina, and their two young children lived in a suburb forty minutes away by car if you were lucky with traffic, well over an hour if you weren't. He'd tried to convince me to live out there as well, but I'd chosen Kypseli because I'd grown up here and couldn't imagine living anywhere else.

"It's okay," he said before I answered. "You're jet-lagged. She'll understand, but you have to visit this week."

George left, pleased that I was satisfied with his apartment choice. I slipped off the blue, curlicued ribbon from around the box and found that it was full of cookies, almond twists dusted with powdered sugar and pieces of crushed pistachio, the kind sold by the kilogram at bakeries.

I hung my clothes in a closet that smelled strongly of mothballs. While I was debating if I should eat the box of cookies for dinner, someone knocked on my door. It was

Maria, holding a plate covered in tinfoil. "Eat," she said, and left without much more conversation. I peeled back the foil and there were two peppers and a tomato glistening in a pool of reddish oil, the vegetables stuffed with rice and ground beef.

That evening I sat at the desk with the food and wondered if it had been a good idea to rent this apartment. I was living only two blocks away from my childhood home. I'd walked on this street dozens of times and passed this exact building, but I'd never conceived that one day I might be living in it. My childhood self would've laughed. My twenty-year-old self would've punched me in the face. But over the years my priorities had shifted, and returning to Greece now, in my fifties, seemed like the natural progression of things.

When I accepted the job at Calypso, I didn't think twice about renting an apartment in Kypseli even though, logically, I should've chosen an apartment closer to the office, across the city and by the port in Piraeus. Since I wasn't leasing a car, my commute would involve a bus, a subway and a ten-minute walk. But Kypseli had always been my home, and it could be fun, I'd thought, to get back to my roots. As it got dark outside, I realized that there was something melancholy about being back, this time alone, my wife and daughter in Canada as if they'd never happened to me. My parents dead. I'd sold their apartment when they'd died, even though everyone had told me to hang on to it. I could've rented it out, like my landlord in Chicago, but at the time I'd ignored this advice, eager to be free from any additional burden heaped on my shoulders by my parents.

At the very least, I could've picked a location with fewer emotional associations. Maria's food was better than anything my mother had ever cooked, but I had the vague sensation of being a child again, as if my mother was in the tiny kitchen waiting for me to finish so that she could swoop up the dishes and send me off to bed. I hadn't anticipated that feeling. Of being watched.

Back in Canada, the act of remembering my life in Greece in detail had been impossible. I could perhaps conjure a tone or an emotion, but specific memories blurred. Now flashbacks came in, pointed and quick. I could remember entire conversations I hadn't considered in more than twenty years. Craving the present tense, I picked up the phone to call Toronto. Anna answered after the second ring.

"Zoe was worried that you didn't call sooner," she said.

"I was unpacking. I wanted to settle in first."

"And now you're settled?"

"More or less. How are you?"

"Fine."

This kind of clipped conversation had become our norm over the past few months, and it was disappointing to see it transposed to our first telephone call.

"Are you sure you're fine?"

"Why don't you talk to Zoe?"

I'd wanted to talk to Anna for longer, but a conversation with Zoe would be lighter. She was shy when she picked up the receiver, and I had to ask question after question to coax words out of her. I knew she'd relaxed when she asked what movie I'd watched on the plane.

When I hung up, it was close to midnight. I turned off the lights in the apartment and lay down in the bed, which I discovered was actually two single beds pushed together and covered in a single queen-sized sheet. I slept on the side I did back home, the left.

The bedroom had a small balcony, just big enough for me to stand on, and even though the evenings in February were chilly, I'd left the door open to air out the apartment's mustiness. Despite the time, there was still activity outside. A television blaring from another apartment, someone laughing. The sounds wove together into a blanket of sleep-inducing white noise.

I'd planned on spending my first few days back in Athens getting organized. I had to go to the bank, stock up my apartment, get reacquainted with public transportation. I'd arrived on a Saturday, and on Sunday, almost everything was closed and I couldn't accomplish much, so I ventured out into the neighbourhood instead.

Until my parents died, I'd visited them once or twice a year, and during those short two-week trips, my journeys always had a purpose: to see a specific person, to buy something from a store or pharmacy, to pay a bill at the bank. I was too preoccupied to pay attention to my surroundings. Now that I was back in Kypseli and had some time to dawdle, I was alert, looking for signs of—what? That things had changed? Stayed the same?

Everything was dirtier. On my walk I noticed cat shit smeared on sidewalks and counted more than a few rivulets of water of dubious origin streaming down the streets and pooling into fetid puddles. The garbage bins were often overflowing, small, stuffed plastic bags scattered around them like someone had been playing basketball and repeatedly missed the hoop. Some parked cars hadn't been driven in months; you could tell by the dirt that clung to their windows, textured like mould.

There were stores where there hadn't been stores before,

most of them closed, and restaurants, even if they'd remained in the same spot, had different names.

It was noisier, too, and during the day, the sounds of the city multiplied exponentially. First the birds woke up at the crack of dawn. I was used to pigeons, but canaries were new. People kept them in cages on their balconies and they tweeted high and fast, more like hamsters treading un-greased wheels than birds. There was a slew of sounds relating to cars—bursts of alarms, minor traffic jams that made drivers lean on their horns and yell out their windows. Once or twice a day trucks would make their way slowly through the streets selling vegetables or furniture, the driver describing their wares through old, half-broken loudspeakers. I'd forgotten about the noise, the sheer accumulation of it.

I found a café and ordered coffee. The waitress told me where I could get a few groceries on a Sunday, and I bought some food for dinner before returning to my apartment.

My balcony was covered in a thick layer of city dust and pigeon droppings, and before eating outside I sloshed buckets of soapy water across the floor. The balconies in the apartment building across from mine were lush with potted plants tall enough to give their owners a modicum of privacy. I would catch glimpses of people's feet or the tops of their heads poking out behind the shrubs. My balcony, on the other hand, was barren. I set up a small plastic table I'd found folded up in the closet and dragged out one of the kitchen table chairs, but that was the extent of my outdoor furnishing.

My balcony was separated from Maria and Spiro's by a sheet of frosted glass. I could see the shadowy forms of their bodies and I could hear them, too, but the conversations I overheard were one-sided, one of them yelling to the other from the inside.

While I was eating my first solo meal, Spiro spied my silhouette.

"Hey, friend," he called over the partition. "Everything okay?"

"I can't complain."

He leaned over the railing and around the partition. He had a drooping grey moustache. "Maria told me about you yesterday."

"Nice to meet you."

"Welcome to the neighbourhood. You must join us for dinner tonight."

I gestured to my plate. "I got hungry early; I've already served myself."

"Tomorrow, then."

"I might be having dinner with my cousins," I said, even though George and I had decided to meet later in the week.

"So busy already! We don't want to bother you."

It was a bad move, I knew, to possibly offend the two people I'd see most. "I can reschedule. I'd love to have dinner with you and Maria."

I darted inside to get my phone number since I didn't have it memorized yet, but when I stepped back onto the balcony and called out his name, he was gone. Of course. He didn't need my number; he was just going to yell for me when it was time to come over. I was back in Greece again.

ZOE

I met Hugo two months after moving to Montreal for university. The temperature had been hovering around zero all day and I'd seen some flurries here and there, but I was still hanging on to the last days of fall. I walked through Parc La Fontaine and sat down at a lone picnic table. The rest were stored away, so to find one seemed auspicious. I ignored the cold leaching through my jeans and opened my journal to write a poem, but doodled a picture of the man-made pond in the middle of the park instead. It had been drained for the season, so it was just a big, gravelly basin.

Hugo came up behind me and looked over my shoulder. "Isn't it too cold to draw outside?" He spoke to me in French first, and then switched to English when I didn't respond right away.

My fingers were bright pink from the wind and my nose was running. "Not really," I said.

"Are you an artist or something?"

I shook my head again. "I'm Zoe."

He walked away, but returned a few minutes later, holding two small stones.

"You should use these to weigh down the corners of your pages when it's windy." He gave them to me and they were round and heavy for their size, like overripe lemons, still warm from his hands.

When he invited me to his apartment, I wasn't afraid

or hesitant to accept. I marvelled instead at how I'd never met anyone like this before. It usually happened in a more structured way, direct lines connecting person to person: through school, friends of friends, the Internet. A chance meeting in a park was thrilling in the way that Montreal had seemed thrilling the first time I visited and decided I should move for school. My meeting with Hugo confirmed the magical status I'd always suspected the city had.

We bought a bottle of cheap wine from the dep around the corner and sat on his living room floor and talked. We got drunk quickly, and he turned sweet and started calling me a rotation of names. *Baby, honey*. Darling, but with the *g* dropped and a Southern accent. *Darlin'*. I was Zoe only once and that was when we were in bed, his eyes first closed and later open. He said my name and then he came and we fell asleep tangled up, damp and sticky.

I woke up in the middle of the night, Hugo's lanky body sprawled out beside mine. He was tall and skinny, six-three, all bowed legs and noodly arms, more than a foot taller than me. He had this hair. It billowed around his head, frizzy and curly, a golden halo crowning his pointed face. He was snoring and I couldn't get back to sleep, so I went to the bathroom. I opened the medicine cabinet, half-expecting to find a stockpile of pills, but instead of drugs, I found hair products: aerosol cans of hairspray; pump bottles of two different kinds of gel. I opened a jar of moulding mud and smoothed its creamy contents onto my own hair. It smelled like flowers, like a manufactured spring breeze. I looked at myself in the mirror and my cheeks were flushed and my hair looked shiny, not in a greasy way, but in a styled, pretty way.

Hugo was awake when I went back to bed. We kept talking, and he told me about his sister, Chantal. When she was eight years old she went on a school trip at a sugar shack and jumped on one of the big workhorses when no one was looking. The horse got spooked, and as she fell off, it kicked her forehead. She died from the impact.

Hugo had been at school writing a history test. He hadn't studied and spent most of the class trying to peek at the answers of the girl beside him, but she noticed and blocked her paper. Instead of muddling through the remaining questions on his own, he just looked out the window. He said it was snowing, so he watched the tumbling flakes—they were the big, fluffy kind—and then, right before the class ended, he was called to the principal's office. He thought he was getting in trouble for cheating.

I've always hated exchanging stories of deaths, and what I liked about moving away was that no one knew anything about my background. My father drowned when a freak storm blew over the small boat he'd rented while on a vacation in Greece. It was a story that was easy to pass around, students sitting idly in the cafeteria, eating pizza and talking about the weirdest things closest to their real lives. My story was weird and real, and it was a defining characteristic. For years, people would see my picture in the yearbook and remember me as *that* girl.

When Hugo brought up Chantal, he had no idea about any of this. He told me about her because, he said, he'd gotten a good vibe from me at the park. Hugo was interested in energy and described people according to it, the same way someone might mention a hair colour or height. My energy, apparently, was warm and gentle and trusting.

As much as I hated to admit it, my father's death was an important part of me, and lying beside Hugo, I was overcome with the desire for him to know my important parts, every single one of them. So I responded to his story about Chantal by telling him about my dad.

My father immigrated to North America from Greece when he was in his late twenties, first to the United States and then to Canada. When I was thirteen, he went back to Greece. It was only supposed to be temporary, a mission to rescue the shipping business my great-grandfather had founded a century earlier. After he left, I talked to him often, three or four times a week. The Internet wasn't a big thing yet, so we relied on the telephone and the first time we spoke, I didn't recognize his voice. He'd always had an accent, but I was so accustomed to it that it never registered as foreign. On the phone, his presence distilled to a disembodied voice, I heard it for it was: he sounded like a stranger. During our last conversation, he said he was going to book a ticket for me to visit him, but three days later, he had his accident.

"That's horrible." Hugo's forehead was resting on my arm, his hair tickling me.

"Thank you," I said. I wasn't sure what else to say.

We spent the rest of the weekend together, sometimes drifting off to sleep, sometimes awake and talking, and after that day, I rarely slept in my own bed.

I didn't believe in love at first sight, but I did believe in love as a leaping flame, a freshly struck match. When it came I was convinced it came suddenly, in one initial, spectacular blinding. I was sure that what I felt about Hugo wasn't infatuation or naïveté or desperation; it was simply a beginning.

When I first moved to Montreal, my roommate, Susie, and I got drunk with a bunch of other students we'd just met. That evening, I pictured my undergrad life: trudging to the library during massive snowstorms, drinking the same watered down beer at the bar with these new friends, staying up all night to write a paper or to exchange drunken, sloppy opinions. I imagined I would become deeply absorbed in my studies and read Victorian novels for my English degree and write my first volume of poetry in my spare time. I didn't mind my single bed, the shared bathrooms, the lack of privacy.

In reality, my classes were kind of boring. They were all at the introductory level and there were so many students in them that it was hard to strike up conversations. I'd take a seat at the back of the room and slip out as soon as a lecture was over. I'd moved to Montreal craving something different, transformative, and at first I thought the experience of attending university would be enough, but then I met Hugo.

He was older than me, twenty-three, and he was a painter or at least wanted to be one. When he wasn't painting, he worked at a café. He'd lived in the same apartment since he was eighteen and the rent had barely increased. It was a studio, long and skinny like him, the sleeping area at one end, the kitchen in the middle, and a living room at the front. When I'd come over, we'd hang out in the living room, the only room that got direct sunlight, and he'd show me the progress he'd made on a painting.

I was more interested in writing poems, so instead of studying, I would take out my notebook or laptop and write while Hugo painted. He didn't have an Internet connection, so I had no choice but to write. The scratched hardwood floors gleamed in the sunlight and it was comforting sitting there on cold winter afternoons, the two of us talking about the meaning of his art or me shyly reading out my poetry, our socked feet pressing against the slick floors.

All of my poems were about love, which by default meant they were about Hugo. I was going through an E.E. Cummings phase and wrote about bodies and used too many parentheses. Hugo was painting trees. Their souls, he said. His paintings were mainly abstract, rusty hues of paint scraped into swirls with stiff brushes or palettes, and they would dry into glossy, textured pieces that I would touch lightly afterwards, exactly what you're not allowed to do in an art gallery.

I wanted Hugo to paint me and often after having sex, I would lie naked on my side and try to position myself so that he would feel inspired by my body, the curves of my limbs. If I leaned a certain way, I knew my breasts looked better, but no matter how much I posed, he didn't paint me. We went to the Musée des beaux-arts once and there was an Egon Schiele painting of a prostitute, one of his angular, bug-eyed nudes, and more than any of the other paintings of naked women, I was jealous of that model and that she'd been chosen.

I suppose that even if Hugo didn't paint me, he knew how to kiss, and sometimes that was enough, or too much, depending on how I was feeling. When I couldn't think of anything to write, I'd look at his assembly of paints. If I were to paint him, I'd use only yellows and oranges and reds. A fiery sunset, a flaming prairie.

ANNA

I lived in France for three months when I was twenty-two, just after I'd graduated from university. Today even a single month passes in an instant—you blink and it's over—but those weeks stretched into a lifetime. My parents coordinated the trip, bought me the plane ticket and gave me spending money. I even had an entire apartment to myself. It belonged to a co-worker of my father's. He normally rented it out, fully furnished, but had a gap between tenants, and he let me live in it in exchange for watering the plants and keeping it clean. It was tiny and perfect, a studio on Rue Perronet, just off Boulevard St. Germain.

I knew one person in the entire city, a friend from school named Hélène, who had studied in Toronto for a year. I called her when I found out I'd be going and she visited me on my first night. We smoked off my tiny balcony. There was only enough space for one chair, so we stood with our arms slung over the sides of the wrought-iron bars and waited until her boyfriend picked us up. Jean-François drove a rusted forest-green Citroën and he insisted I sit in the front, since I was the guest. He brought us down the Champs-Elysées and when we passed the Eiffel Tower, it was dark and shadowy, its outline twinkling with little lights. Jean-François kept taking detours through the narrowest streets or slowing down to point out different landmarks, some touristy, like Notre-Dame Cathedral, some important only to him (his dentist), while other cars honked their horns behind us. If it hadn't been for Hélène's hovering cigarette smoke, I would've forgotten she was with us in the back seat.

The next evening, Jean-François came over uninvited, alone. I was sitting on the balcony—I spent most of my time there—and he honked from the street. I yelled at him to come up.

Jean-François spoke broken English and I spoke broken French, and we spent hours talking to each other, teasing the other person's attempts at their language. *I love you*, he said, and I hit him on the arm.

One weekend he drove me to his parents' home in a town called Langres, which is known for a particular type of pungent cheese that I only pretended to like and then one day did like, but only when I was older and no longer in contact with him. We passed champagne vineyards on the way over, golden and pale green fields stretching out like squares on a quilt, and I still remember how peaceful I felt when I realized we'd left behind the grey sprawl of Paris. It was as if the peacefulness were an entity unto itself, gently blanketing me.

Langres is surrounded by high stone ramparts, and Jean-François took me for a walk along them at dusk. We saw large flocks of swallows darting back and forth above us, looking like they were going to smash headfirst into the walls, but at the last minute they swooped gracefully, impossibly, into small crevices hidden in the stones.

On our way back to Paris, Jean-François took a detour along a mountain road. Halfway up we stopped to see the view and, while we were outside, I heard a soft clanging noise. I thought of a marching band or an ice-cream truck. We got back in the car and drove to the highest point and found a herd of cows in a field of soft yellow-green grass. The clanging had been their cowbells.

I saw Hélène a few times before I left and she didn't know I was sleeping with Jean-François, but she talked about how she never saw him anymore and that he was a bastard and that she was through with him.

The snapshots I have from the trip were taken by Jean-François: me in front of the Eiffel Tower, me standing along the ramparts in Langres, me on the side of the road with the cows in the background. I made a few passing references to Jean-François in the letters I wrote back home, but they were so subtle that for all intents and purposes, our relationship could've never happened. There's no proof of it.

I'd been thinking recently about the importance of telling stories and talking about memories. If they weren't shared and if there wasn't tangible evidence of them, what was the proof that they'd ever actually existed or occurred?

I was also thinking about Jean-François because I was on a plane headed to Paris. The last time I flew was when Niko died and Zoe and I went to Greece for the funeral. That was six years ago, and it felt just as long ago, just as recent, as that trip to Paris when I was twenty-two.

Daniel planned the trip. We'd talked about taking a vacation for months and he was the one who finally did something about it. He bought the tickets without telling me; he just forwarded me the itinerary while I was at work, with the subject line *Surprise*! In the e-mail he wrote, *These tickets are non-refundable so you're going to find a way to go no matter what.*

I was nervous about the flight when the plane taxied down the runway and the lights went off in the cabin. I hadn't expected it and the darkness made me think, for a second, that something was wrong. We were seated above the wheels and I could feel the whirr and crunch of gears beneath me. I closed my eyes and reached for Daniel's hand.

When the plane stabilized and the seat-belt sign clicked off, I opened my eyes again. I was always slightly relieved when I noticed I still had the capacity to be surprised. For a while nothing surprised me, and I didn't think anything would ever again. Even the most horrible things—earthquakes levelling cities, sinkholes opening up and swallowing houses and their inhabitants, planes exploding on takeoff: these kinds of events made me sad, but they didn't surprise me. Of course they happened, I told myself; the world was unpredictable and cruel and any number of things could go wrong at any moment.

It was like I'd been dulled, nerves cauterized and accustomed to electric shocks so that they'd barely quiver when the voltage got cranked up. I expected things to occur, good and bad, and when they did, an event out of the ordinary, it was a confirmation of my expectations. The fear that it would happen again, that I'd be engulfed in numbness, hovered at the back of my mind.

I spent the first years of my life in a house near Kirkland Lake, where my father worked as a mine geologist. When my mother talked about those years, she never failed to bring up the fact that we lived in a cottage, not a house. There was a clear distinction. A cottage was a place best suited for summer vacations and two-week stretches at Christmas, if you were feeling ambitious. It was not meant for year-long living, and certainly not for half a decade. The owners of the cottage rented it to the company my father worked for, and we lived in it for free as part of his salary package. There was a wood stove and a seemingly self-replenishing stack of firewood piled high outside. During the coldest parts of winter, we had to keep the faucets on a trickle overnight to prevent them from freezing. "It would be quaint if it wasn't home," my father would say as consolation, even though he, unlike my mother, loved living there.

He enjoyed the quiet of our rural home, and in the winter, liked the feeling of his family barricaded as one against the snow, the harsh climate. His career was built on examining the particular geographies of the Canadian landscape, so he respected them, was humbled by them in a way most people can't seriously muster, but when he was offered a research position back in Toronto, he knew he had to accept it. We never returned, not even for a visit. My mother refused.

I can still easily conjure up an image of the lake. How big it was. I visited the area one more time when I was older, just Niko and I, not knowing I was a few weeks pregnant with Zoe and had mistaken my exhaustion and vague nausea for the effects of fresh air and nostalgia. The lake still looked as vast as it had to me as a small child.

I remember the lake most clearly in the summer, the darkness of that water until you peered in and saw that it wasn't actually opaque, but clear and dark green, and that there were things floating in it, particles and feathery plants and sometimes, if you were lucky, a small swarm of fish, like little flecks of gold that your father could catch and show you.

I would dip my toes into the water slowly and jump back as the cold shot up my leg and into my body. I remember walking along the dock, the shuffle of dry, bare feet on wood, my mother holding my hand. I got a splinter once and my father extracted it with a hot needle, holding my foot firmly with one hand while he prodded it out with the other. And there were so many pine trees! A giant mass of them surrounding us, and the smell of fallen needles on the ground everywhere. Stepping on them barefoot was like being nipped by invisible mites. I didn't talk much when I was there; I screamed and yelped and laughed in delight instead.

Years later my parents' basement flooded, and although the majority of the items destroyed were junk, the photo album from those years was also ruined. I was with my mother when she found the waterlogged book, the pages swollen, smelling murky and mouldy. She flipped it open and I was surprised when she cried instantly, the loss of those pictures and that time.

My parents are now dead, so they can't vouch for me anymore, for my existence between the ages of zero and five. The photos have been ruined for years; Zoe has never seen what I looked like as a baby. Before she moved to Montreal, I kept meaning to tell her what I remembered about those years, but I wasn't sure why it would matter when there were so many other things I should've told her first.

Maybe it doesn't matter what memories are shared or what photographs are taken. Whatever happens shapes me as an individual, and how I'm shaped affects the people I know, and how I react in given circumstances. Maybe that's all that counts, that's sufficient proof.

NIKO

During my first week back, I visited the cargo port where some of Calypso's ships were docked. I was eager for the job to feel real and thought seeing something with their logo would help. The industrial port was in Keratsini Bay, just west of the passenger port in Piraeus. I left Kypseli and took the subway across the city. I wasn't sure how to get to Keratsini Bay and could've taken a cab to save time, but I preferred figuring it out on my own, like a puzzle.

Since the 1950s, Athens had started to sprawl outwards into a repetitive copy-paste of the same kind of scenery, regardless of the neighbourhood, and I was reminded of it as I squinted at street signs through the bus window. We passed the same buildings, the same small streets, the same cars and garbage bins I saw in Kypseli. People who aren't familiar with Athens have a more romantic view of the city. They picture the Acropolis, the ancient agora, marbled sidewalks, but it's actually much uglier than that. There's traffic, smog and dirt, and harried people who don't apologize when they bump into you. There's heat and bad odours and cockroaches scuttling around in the dark.

I got off the bus and walked toward Keratsini Bay. As I approached, the sidewalk turned into what seemed like a highway median, and cars whizzed by me on both sides at top speed. Every so often, I'd step over dried-out dog shit or wooden boards with protruding rusty nails. When

I reached the port, I couldn't figure out how to bypass the gates blocking the water's edge.

I came across a small church, though. It was the size of a walk-in closet, large enough for one person at a time. I went inside and sat on the single chair in front of the small altar. There were some burnt-out candles, but I didn't have a lighter to get them going again, so I dropped a coin in a collection box and hoped it would help me get closer to the ships. An icon of St. Nicholas, the patron saint of sailors, stared at me. Nicholas was my namesake saint, as well my grandfather's, my great-grandfather's, and that of an even longer line before them. This string of names in a family was sometimes comforting and sometimes oppressive. When it came time to name Zoe, it had been thrilling to break from tradition and choose a new name instead of my mother's, even though, after I told her over the phone, she'd cried in disappointment.

Nearby, a man was selling grilled meat and drinks to people on lunch breaks. I bought two skewers and a Coke. "How do I get in there?" I asked, and gestured to the gates.

"Ask someone to let you in," he suggested. "Or just go. No one will stop you."

I ate and drank and then did as he said. It wasn't actually very hard to slip through, and when a security guard yelled at me, I just ignored him and kept walking.

The ships in port were either empty and ready to be loaded down or waiting for the okay to leave. Containers dangled from cranes while men barked directions for their landing. I couldn't see anything belonging to Calypso, but finally this was something: the sea! Massive ships! This was why I'd come here. I leaned against a metal column and breathed in the clouds of diesel fumes. I was sweating, but satisfied.

Even though Calypso's owners had hired me to work for them, the company had originated with my family on my father's side in the late 1800s. My grandfather and his two brothers formally started the business on the island of Spetses. They named it after themselves, Kiriakos Maritime Lines, and their first fleet consisted of two modest fishing boats. It expanded over time, enough to justify a move toward Athens and the main port in Piraeus. At KML's peak, they had seven ships—some passenger ferries and dry bulk containers. The company wasn't exceptionally big, but it did well for its size.

As the founding brothers got older, they drafted succession plans. Among them were three sons and three daughters. The girls were either too young or not interested, and, anyway, they didn't think shipping was a business for women. The boys were my father, his brother, Alexander, and their cousin, John. John knocked himself out of the running early after his parents divorced and he sided with his mother. Alexander and my father could've easily split the duties between themselves, but my father stated clearly his intentions to focus on a writing career instead of shipping. He didn't want to be tied down to the family business, so Alexander won by default, but he was also, fortunately, most suited to the job.

I'm not sure why my father chose a profession so different from the rest of his family. He fought for it, though—while he called himself a writer, his identity card said otherwise, and according to the state he was an accountant, which was funny since he was horrible with money. He'd either forced himself or was coerced into studying it in school, but after graduating did everything he could to avoid that fate.

He couldn't leave the family business completely behind,

though. When he was between writing jobs and in a bind, Alexander would find some bookkeeping work for him to do to at KML to justify a paycheque without bruising his ego. There would be months-long stretches when he wouldn't set foot in the office, but then an expense would come up and my parents would huddle around the drawer in the bedroom where they hid some savings and my father would take the bus down to Piraeus to talk.

When I was growing up, Alexander seemed like the ideal man, a giant or god compared with my father. He had the aura of a captain about him, and in the majority of the photos I have, he's standing on one of the ships, water looming in the background. My parents used to tell me that literature would open the world to me, that I could learn anything and everything by reading through the stacks of novels they kept in the apartment, but it was Alexander who made the world outside my neighbourhood tempting.

He gave me an atlas once, a handsome hardcover book with maps of the entire world. It was a maritime atlas, so it highlighted the world in terms of ports. Those with dry-dock facilities were underlined twice; they were important. There was an inset map for Piraeus, but not the rest of Athens, and I could find the exact coordinates of where my uncle lived, but nothing for me and my parents downtown. I studied the page with North America the most, learned the names New York, Philadelphia, Boston, Charleston, Savannah, Jacksonville. Canada was Montreal, Toronto, and a place called Moose Factory, and then there were insets of Nova Scotia and New Brunswick and the St. Lawrence Seaway. Soon after moving to Toronto, I had to drive to Montreal for work, and was pleased when I finally saw the St. Lawrence River in real life. I remembered it as the skinny pathway rendered in the maritime atlas I had studied so intently when I was a child.

Alexander was hard-working, and while I think my father worked hard, too, it wasn't in a way that made sense to me. Alexander clearly respected the fact that his role was to provide for his family. He understood that there was pleasure to be derived from being a boss and owning a business. My father's pleasures were different, harder to comprehend.

When I was eight years old, Alexander told me that he was taking over the business from my grandfather. He was wearing a suit. My father hadn't anticipated his visit and was wearing slacks and an undershirt. My mother was out.

"You can be in charge, too," I said to my dad, and he laughed. Alexander had laughed, too, but I was humiliated. Not for what I'd said, but for my father's reaction. It seemed disrespectful of him to sit there, skinny, half-dressed, and laugh at Alexander's job.

Growing up, people would tell me when they'd come across my father's writing in a newspaper. They were always complimentary and, without fail, said that, with those genes, I must do well in my own composition classes. I didn't do well in composition class and I didn't know what to do with these compliments, but I learned how to smile politely and say thank you. As I got older, I grew wary of the compliments since even after years of them, they never added up to anything like what we could have amassed with Alexander and the family business. I was becoming aware of how much shabbier our apartment was compared to his. It was small and dark and always cluttered with books and papers, unlike his, which was decorated tastefully with items purchased abroad.

When I first moved I would often tell people that my

family was involved in shipping, which in turn made them think my life back in Greece was glamorous. Niarchos, Onassis, Livanos—these names represented people who were rich and beautiful, who were friends with royalty and celebrities, who bought entire islands to vacation on. Their lifestyles were not at all similar to my life in Athens, but the names were mythological, and I would throw them around casually as if we were somehow linked. As my life became more established in North America, I didn't need the crutch of a fictional glamorous life back in Greece and stopped talking about anything to do with ships.

When KML was sold out of the family, I didn't complain. I thought it was a shame, but I also understood. Alexander had guided the company until he was just shy of sixty and by then it had grown enough that the majority of the employees were no longer relatives, and those who were worked only in administration. The actual shipping crew was left to strangers. When he retired, he sold his ownership to an outside partner, who then sold it to the current owners, the ones who hired me, a pair of brothers named Jimmy and Christos. They'd promptly changed the name from Kiriakos Maritime Lines to Calypso in an effort to rebrand into something more internationally friendly.

With Alexander's sale, KML was officially out of our bloodline. For a while there were some second or third cousins who continued working for the new owners, but I didn't know them, and at a certain point a cousin is meaningless until you need them for a favour. Their numbers also dwindled as the years progressed and their children moved into other industries.

The only person betrayed by Alexander's sale of KML was my father, even though he'd spent most of his life struggling to distance himself from it. Right before Alexander made the sale, my father called me in Toronto. He never called—I was the one who made long-distance phone calls—and the first thing I thought was that my mother had died. Instead he just wanted to tell me about Alexander's intentions.

"Are you thinking of buying it yourself?" I asked.

"No," my father said. "I just thought you'd want to know."

I could hear a *told you so* tone through the bad telephone connection, but I didn't consider what Alexander had done a betrayal. I knew he had his reasons. The company was too small to have any real clout. The fleet had been sold off over the years and what remained was old and would have to be replaced sooner than later. Alexander didn't have the capital or energy to improve the company, and his two children weren't interested in shipping, so rather than saddle them with a dying business, he cut the ties, made a profit. By then I was making a name for myself at my job in Canada, Zoe was a toddler, Anna was starting her career. I didn't feel as though I was being cheated out of anything.

No one, not even my father, would have predicted that I'd be back in Athens, working for Calpyso, years later. The desire came to me slowly, an accumulation of small ideas rather than springing from my head as a fully formed being with breastplate. I was getting older and I'd started thinking about legacy, about what I'd leave behind for Zoe. I'd been working at my job for more than fifteen years and it was going well enough. I didn't work long hours, my salary was good and I had a clear career trajectory until the day I retired. It wasn't exciting, but at least it was consistent and reliable, although it increasingly felt like it wasn't enough.

It started when my mother died, a year after my father. Alexander was already gone, dead years earlier from a heart attack. I remember being confused by how he'd managed to outlive my father. Alexander was not the kind of businessman to get soft in the belly with money. He didn't deny himself his food and drink, but he took care of himself, and was strong. I'd always made sure to see him when I was in Athens, and even though he was only a little younger than my father, the difference in their appearance was palpable. My father gave the impression that he was crumbling with age, like disintegrating newspaper clippings.

My father's death was less of a shock, and when my mother called to tell me, I knew before she even said the words. A nurse from the senior citizens home was the one who told me about my mother. It was six in the morning in Toronto and Anna and I were still in bed. Zoe answered since she was going through a phase where she was waking up early ("To watch the sunrise," she said, but really she was watching cartoons; she'd gotten an idea from somewhere that there was something romantic about watching the sun come up). She came to our room, crying. The nurse had barked the few English words she knew over and over again: "She's dead, she's dead, she's dead." I admonished the nurse for traumatizing Zoe, and when I hung up the phone, realized that my strongest ties to the city were really and truly gone.

I flew to Athens by myself to take care of my mother's funeral arrangements. The funeral was small and I'd been happy to see George. One afternoon we sat for hours in a tavern near my parents' apartment, drinking ouzo and catching up. Because he was a doctor and his practice was in Piraeus, he had some patients who were involved in the shipping industry. He was a cousin on my mother's side, but he'd always known about KML and then Calypso and had kept tabs on the company over the years. Recently there had been some gossip that they were going through a rough patch and were perhaps looking to hire some new personnel. He hadn't expected me to show interest in the details, but I did. Seeing all those names etched into a neat column in the marble of our family tomb had rattled me. The ouzo made it worse.

George gave me the phone number of one of the owners, Jimmy, and I had a coffee with him before returning to Toronto. They were indeed looking for new staff, he told me. Not right away, but if their strategy went according to plan, they might need new management in the future. I chalked up the meeting to healthy curiosity, nothing more, and didn't even mention it to Anna. For the remainder of my stay I continued with the process of selling my parents' apartment, closing their accounts and generally removing any evidence of them from the realm of the living, but I filed the possibility of one day working for Calypso in the back of my mind.

When I returned to Toronto, I couldn't quell the ideas raised by my meeting with Jimmy. One night, unable to sleep, I got up, went to my office in the basement and shut the door. It wouldn't hurt, I thought, to get a few more details. To weigh my options. It was morning in Athens, so I called Jimmy's office number.

"Realistically," I asked, "what are the odds of me working for you?" The negotiations began.

We had a few more phone calls and I was confident that Jimmy was seriously considering hiring me. His brother was more of an investor than an active participant in the day-to-day operations and would agree with whatever Jimmy decided. So, I brought it up with Anna.

"We can all move to Greece," I said. "Isn't that great?"

She'd been smiling the whole time I told her about my late-night conversations, but when I was finished she stopped.

"You really want to quit your job here to work in Greece?"

"Well, I'm thinking about it."

"To work at a company called Calypso."

"Yes."

"Do you know who Calypso even is?"

"What do you mean?"

"Mythologically."

"I know who she is."

"Tell me."

"She's a sea goddess. Odysseus lived on her island for years. She was good in bed, and she wanted to turn him into a god and make him her husband, but he whined and returned to Penelope. Eventually."

"He didn't just live with her, she kept him hostage."

"No one's taking me hostage. I'm going by choice. If I'm going. I don't know, it was just an idea. They don't have a position for me yet."

"But if they do have one, you're going to go?"

"Maybe. What do you think—should I?"

"I think that if you leave, you're not going to come back," she said.

I moved back to Greece two years after my first conversation with Jimmy. He hired me as the vice-president of finance even though I didn't have any formal background in finance—I got my master's degree in engineering, and almost got my PhD, but then started working when I moved to Canada and abandoned school. But I'd spent a lot of time on budgets at my job and Calypso needed someone with international experience. I was good with a calculator and I understood how things worked, but most importantly, my grandfather had founded the business years and years earlier. That counted for something. I wanted to work for Calypso to pay my debts to the sea, to my grandfather, to Alexander and, I suppose, to my father as well. To let them know that the company was not in vain, that my father's late change of heart wasn't an empty gesture.

By the time I joined, Jimmy and Christos were in the midst of refocusing. Their goal was to delve deeper into shipping consultation, to outsource. They had some new ad copy written that made mention of my grandfather and great-uncles:

> *Our mission is to continue in the illustrious tradition of our forefathers, and also to live up to the requirements of modern maritime enterprises.*

I would follow in the footsteps of my forefathers as well, even if I was a little late.

ZOE

Winter settled into Montreal, and my daily routine revolved around Hugo rather than the friendships I'd started back in the fall. His apartment was so warm and easy to escape to. I would get texts from Susie sometimes, like *Yo, are you still alive?* or *How's your imaginary boyfriend?* She referred to him as imaginary since I still hadn't introduced them. I wasn't in a hurry to introduce Hugo to anyone; he was a separate, distinct part of my life. His friends were older and francophone and I didn't spend much time with them either. I'd catch glimpses of what we looked like together and we were a little ridiculous—he was so much taller than me, and his hair was so unruly—but it also made us special. We were a self-contained unit.

A few weeks after Christmas, my mother called and said she was going to visit for the weekend. She suggested taking me and Hugo out to dinner and I hesitated before agreeing.

"You get to meet my mother," I told him that night.

"I do?" He was in bed, reading a magazine.

"She'll be here this weekend."

"Here?"

"Well, at a hotel."

"Oh," he said, and kept reading. "I hate meeting people's parents."

"You'll like her."

He made a face.

"Please?" I'd assumed that eventually meeting my mother was a natural part of the trajectory of our relationship, so why not a little sooner than expected?

He looked up from the magazine. "Fine."

Hugo wasn't close to his parents. My mother and I had gravitated toward each other after my father's death, but Hugo had distanced himself from his, who, unable to cope with the sprawling sadness associated with Chantal's death, became crazy in a way that pushed him away. They were concerned with two things: whether Chantal was safe and happy in the afterworld and what they had done to deserve her death, as if it could've been prevented by good behaviour. They shopped around for opinions. First they went to a medium who, with the help of one of Chantal's unwashed T-shirts, fell into a trance when she attempted to make contact with her in the realm of the spirits. Hugo imitated the medium's voice for me—low and reedy and definitely otherworldly. Chantal was fine, she told them.

They turned to religion too and concluded that their accumulation of sins had been too great and that Chantal's death had truly been their fault. Less than a year after she died, they sat Hugo down and told him everything they'd ever done wrong: petty theft, instances of gluttony and envy. His father urged him to confess his sins, too, but Hugo couldn't speak. He wracked his brain and couldn't remember anything he'd ever done wrong. What did anyone do to deserve anything? Tears rolled down his parents' cheeks and Hugo just sat there, silent. He knew that his parents could do whatever they wanted and they might get goodness, but they could just as easily get fluky tragedy. It didn't matter. After he moved out, he hardly talked to them, although once a month they sent him a cheque in the mail, enough to cover rent and then some.

As much as I loved every bit of Hugo and told myself I didn't care what my mother thought of him, I cut his hair the day before she arrived. Just a trim, because it was frizzing out into clown-wig territory. We were by the window, and he kept his eyes closed as I snipped the shaggier parts. My hair was slightly longer than his and I would use his mousse to scrunch it up into curls, too. They came out more like frizzy waves, but there was something comforting about matching my boyfriend.

When we were done, he swept the hair off the floor. Later I picked up a lock he'd missed. I recalled my high school geometry class, using a compass to draw perfect circles. His hair, in my hand, curled just like a Fibonacci spiral, the kind of perfection you find only in nature.

Mom took the train from Toronto, and I met her at her hotel downtown in the late afternoon. She wanted to stretch her legs, so we left the warmth of the lobby and walked around the city toward Old Montreal, taking detours until it was time for dinner. I'd left the restaurant's address at Hugo's, but after twenty minutes of waiting, he still hadn't joined us.

"Everything looks so good," Mom said. "Let's just order."

When we finished our appetizers, I stepped outside with the smokers and called him at home. No answer.

"It's me," I said to the voice mail. "Can you call me back?"

I wanted Hugo to get a cell phone like the rest of the world, but he'd just shrug when I suggested it. I waited a few more minutes and tried again. I didn't bother leaving another message.

"It's better that he's not here anyway," Mom said when I

returned. "I have some news."

"What is it?" I sat back in my chair and unwound my scarf.

"I sold the house."

"What?" I thought I'd heard wrong, still distracted by Hugo's no-show.

"It happened quickly—I didn't think it would, but it did."

"You sold it? Just like that? Where are you going to live?" We'd lived in the same house since I was young enough to not remember living anywhere else. Mom had never raised the idea of selling it—not when Dad died, not when I left for school.

"I'll stay with Daniel until I find my own place."

"Why don't you move in with him permanently?"

"I don't know," she said, and laughed a little. "You're the only person I'm used to living with."

Daniel had been my mother's partner for a few years, someone who'd hovered around the periphery of my life until one day I noticed he was truly a part of it, even if he was slightly removed. I probably wouldn't have moved to Montreal if I hadn't known he was there for her. I took him for granted, something solid that blurred into the background, like a hedge. It wasn't the most flattering way to think of someone, as shrubbery, but I didn't dislike him. I just sensed that there was a barrier between us, that the three of us would never be a unit. I didn't want another three-person unit, anyway—I had my own, even if one of the points in the triangle was missing.

"Wow," I said. "When did it sell?"

"I met with the real estate agent just after Christmas, and she suggested putting it up right away, so I went for it. It got multiple offers."

"After *Christmas*?" It was now the middle of February.

"Why didn't you tell me sooner?" I looked down at my food. I'd ordered steak frites and hadn't cut into the meat yet. It looked gross untouched, the pink juices congealing against the sides of the plate.

"I should've, but it was such a whirlwind, and I know you've been busy with school and Hugo. I didn't want to distract you."

"It's my house too."

"I didn't want to upset you either."

"I can handle it."

We each took small bites of our meals. Tears welled up in my eyes and I tried to hold them back, but a few escaped. "I guess I have to pack my things?"

"It's not closing until June, so you have lots of time. I'll take care of everything else."

My mother had a history of withholding information from me. The truth would come out eventually, but it would be delayed, like when she'd waited before telling me that my father had been in his accident. Now she'd spent who knows how long keeping in the information about the house. Even if it had sold quickly, the logic leading up to it must have stretched over weeks, if not months. And we'd spent the day together, walked all over the city, and she hadn't mentioned it. If Hugo had shown up for dinner, would she have waited even longer?

I kept looking down, but I could feel her looking at me, and I knew the exact expression she had on her face, a blend of joy and worry. We knew things about each other, my mother and I, but it was starting to sink in that no matter how close we were or how strong our bond was, there were still myriad ways for her to take me by surprise.

"What are you thinking?" she asked.

I wanted to say that it didn't bother me that she was selling the house I'd grown up in with her and my father. It was kind of true. "I just wish you'd told me sooner," I said instead, which was more true.

"I'm sorry." She reached over the table. "Truly."

"It's okay."

"Let's get dessert, then."

We took a cab back to the hotel and took the elevator up to her room. I stretched out on one of the beds and watched her take off her shoes, remove her earrings. She'd just gotten a haircut, a simple bob. Her hair was normally wavy—she'd started straightening it—and it looked good on her, made her look younger. She was wearing new clothes too. If Hugo had been there, he would've commented on her energy or tried to assign a colour to it, something muddled but intense.

"You should stay here tonight," she said. "You're already comfortable."

After my father died, my mother and I retreated into our own little world. It had already been the two of us when he moved, but our three-minus-one-ness was now official, irrevocable. Often I'd start the night sleeping in my bed, but would wake up hours later and crawl into hers, and she never kicked me out.

"I'm going to a friend's birthday thing," I lied. "I can't miss it, but I'll come over first thing tomorrow."

She rummaged through her purse and handed me the extra hotel key card. "In case you change your mind later."

"Mom, if I snuck into your room at two in the morning, you would freak out."

"Only until I saw it was you."

I went back down to the lobby and sank into one of the big chairs. I wasn't sure what to do with myself. I was nervous to see if Hugo was home and I didn't want to see Susie at the dorm, either.

To bide time, I went to the hotel's basement, but there were only darkened conference rooms, so I took the elevator to the top floor to the pool and gym. The change-room door beeped and clicked open when I held the key card over the sensor. Inside, it was humid and empty, quiet except for my boots squishing on the tiled floor. There was a tall stack of clean, folded towels by the door. I hadn't been swimming once since moving, but I needed to calm down and knew it would tire me out. I could go in my underwear; no one else was around.

I jumped into the pool's deep end, both arms straight in the air. When I was a kid, my father used to tell me that although he knew how to swim, something about living in North America made him forget. He said he couldn't imagine swimming in a pool or a lake and that even the ocean was different from the sea. When I was younger, I was terrified that I would jump into a pool and it would be the day I forgot how to swim, too, but it never happened.

I bobbed back up to the surface, rubbed my eyes and flipped onto my back. The room had a domed white ceiling with a skylight at one end. It was dark outside, and the skylight was just a rectangle of flat winter night sky among the white.

I'm a good swimmer. Not the fastest, but I have endurance, and as part of my swim team when I was younger, I could always be relied on to keep going when everyone else was ready to give up. My best friend, Emily, and I used to spend afternoons in the pool together, and I'd try to teach her how to do the front crawl, but she couldn't even dunk her head underwater without plugging her nose. "How do you do it?" she'd ask, and I would shrug. I just knew.

In the pool, I closed my eyes and wondered if I could fall asleep like this, in the water, on my back. I could just spend the night here, my mother asleep in her hotel room, Hugo in his apartment, Susie with the dorm room to herself for the millionth night. No one would know where I was. But I started thinking about Hugo again and why he hadn't come to dinner. Was he even actually home? He might've missed my note or gotten the dates mixed up. He was scatterbrained sometimes; he wouldn't have done it on purpose. I climbed out of the pool and shimmied back into my clothes, wrung out my wet bra and underwear and stuffed them into the bottom of my bag. I took the bus over and let myself in.

"Your hair's wet," he said when he noticed me. He was working on a painting.

"I went swimming."

"Do you like it?" He gestured to his canvas. Another goddamned tree.

"It's okay." I sat on the couch. A few strands of my hair had frozen and I chewed on them, sucking out the chlorine. "You missed dinner with my mother."

"Sorry. I thought it would be better without me there."

"You should've called me."

"I didn't think you'd notice."

I didn't say anything, and he continued painting while I watched. Finally he stopped and sat next to me. I rested my head on his shoulder.

"I think it would be better if we stopped seeing each other," he said.

"What?" I sat up. "Why?"

"Come on, Zoe."

When Chantal was struck by the horse, she didn't die right away. She was still breathing when the ambulance arrived and she kept breathing for a few more hours afterwards. The doctors couldn't control the swelling of her brain and one by one, her organs started shutting down. When Hugo broke up with me, I thought of little Chantal lying in the hospital, her life slowly extinguishing.

"Listen, I'm sorry," he said, and gently patted the top of my head as if he was my older brother instead of boyfriend.

I spent the night anyway. The next morning I met my mother, but didn't tell her what had happened. If she told me little, I could tell her less, and although I almost faltered when she hugged me goodbye, I didn't cry, not about Hugo or the house or anything.

"Have a good trip home," was all I said before turning around and leaving her.

ANNA

I waffled on what to pack for our vacation—it was March, not quite spring, and I wanted to look nice, but couldn't settle on what was appropriate for the in-between weather. I peeked into Daniel's suitcase and saw that he was bringing running shoes, T-shirts, jeans. He wasn't a very good dresser and this reminder relaxed me. We would be tourists, I told myself, so what.

When I went to Paris at twenty-two, I was deliberate about what I took with me, each piece modelled in front of the full-length mirror in my bedroom from every angle until I was convinced that it was good enough to show off in Europe. Even dresses I thought I loved were analyzed cold and hard. In the end, I was left with such a small assortment of clothes that I was forced to do laundry more often than I'd planned, either handwashing individual items in the small kitchen sink and hanging them out to dry on the tiny balcony, or stuffing everything into a bag and going to the laundromat. There was a fancy cleaner on my street, but the woman who worked there was more stylish than I'd ever be, and I was intimidated. Instead I walked a few blocks away, to a place where I could do it myself for cheap.

I wrote letters back home while my clothes washed. I would sit on one of the uncomfortable chairs by the entrance, wooden with woven twine seats that left indentations on the backs of my legs when I got up. Every single one of my letters was written in that laundromat, although I never mentioned where I was. I hoped they would picture me in the Champs de Mars, my stomach on the grass, or sitting at Les Deux Magots with an espresso and a cigarette. I preferred to go to cafés with Jean-François, to have long conversations rather than being alone and writing. Still, I wanted the recipients of my letters to think I was anywhere but the laundromat with the mint-green walls, spotted linoleum floors and cheap chairs, the air humid and soapy from the machines.

It was usually just me and the older women who lived in the neighbourhood, and while I was busy writing, they would sit there. I never knew how they had the patience to wait without distraction, but these days I find myself doing the same thing. Sitting and enjoying every minute of it, the luxury of quieting my brain. The book I had brought for the flight was still stowed in the compartment above me more than an hour into our flight.

"Look what Steph gave me," Daniel said, and pulled a construction paper card out of the folder on his lap. *Bon Voyage, Daddy*.

"It's adorable." At the bottom of the card she'd written, *I love you!!!!*, and I could picture her dotting those exclamation points with a flourish.

"It's adorable until you turn it over."

I flipped the card and saw a list she'd written of things she wanted him to buy her in Paris. *Merci!*

"Subtle."

"I'm missing a weekend with them. She knows exactly when to ask me for things."

Daniel had two daughters, and of the two, Stephanie and

I got along better. She had welcomed me into her life with a giddy enthusiasm I could only be thankful for. Kelly, who was older, was cooler. She was a few years younger than Zoe, and when we first met, she had a better grasp of my role. She knew I was the one interfering in her parents' relationship and so she worked hard to keep me at arm's length, and I didn't blame her.

Stephanie was all ponytails and giggles, exuberant and a ham. Kelly was haughtier, wore tight T-shirts and leggings, but she would cloak it all with baggy hooded sweatshirts like she wasn't ready to fully reveal herself. She had boots, fake leather, almost up to her knee, and because her legs were so skinny they hung loose around her calves. There was a sexiness about her that so many girls had now, both innocent and dangerous. Zoe hadn't been like either Stephanie or Kelly and I was grateful for that. I was better prepared to handle her personality than Daniel's sexy, shrieking girls.

When we landed at Charles de Gaulle, I was less anxious than I'd been at takeoff because I was in too much of a twilight sleepiness to let any nervousness register. We got off the plane, retrieved our bags and took a long taxi ride to the hotel. It was on Rue Vaneau, in the 7th arrondissement, a nice area, wealthier than where I'd stayed as a student. Our hotel room was on the third floor and there were no elevators. The man who owned the hotel had messy white hair and had to rifle through three drawers before finding our keys, but it was still early enough into the trip that his disorganization was endearing and quintessentially French rather than exasperating. After 10 p.m., he locked the main entrance, so he gave us two keys, a heavy skeleton key for the room and a more modern key for the front door.

Our room was small and the bed took up nearly the entire space. There was a large window that, when the drapes were parted, flooded the room with the most incredible light. We also had a good view into the apartment building across the street. I saw a man sitting at a desk made of glass, leaning back and talking on the phone. He scratched the back of his head and stretched out his arms.

"Is this okay?" Daniel asked.

It was our first trip abroad together, and because Daniel had taken care of most of the arrangements, I could tell he was nervous that I wouldn't like them.

"It's perfect," I assured him, and wrapped my arms around his shoulders.

Daniel was vigilant about jet lag, and before we left he'd purchased melatonin pills from a health-food store that were supposed to help, as if jetlag was a preventable sickness, not the natural result of physically displacing our bodies to a different time zone. He had taken one of the pills on the plane and popped another in the room and offered me the bubble pack.

I declined. "Why don't we lie down instead?"

"No way. You're supposed to stay active as long as possible. I feel good. What about you?"

"I'm hungry. I think."

We left the room in search of food. We could see the Eiffel Tower and, encouraged by Daniel's pills and our mutual travel adrenaline, headed toward it.

Daniel had never been to Paris and at first he expected me to know the way. I thought I should, too, but after two blocks I realized that whatever intuition I might once have had had evaporated. We'd also forgotten our guidebook in the room. At a large, open intersection we saw the Eiffel Tower again, clapped our hands and walked toward it, but as soon as we turned onto a smaller street, it disappeared behind the buildings. Instead of pursuing it, we went to the closest bakery. I wasn't hungry anymore so I just had a few bites of Daniel's baguette while we sat on a bench in a small park where a few children were playing, their parents chatting off to the side, ignoring them. Back at the hotel we cursed the stairs (they had seemed so charming at first!) and then collapsed into bed. It was soft and we sunk in deep.

"We shouldn't sleep just yet," Daniel said. "We'll never go to bed tonight. Let's get up again." His voice was fading.

"Don't worry about it," I told him, but he'd already closed his eyes. He mumbled something incomprehensible. Daniel had a teenage boy's capacity for sleep, and could still sleep in until noon on the weekend if no one was around to wake him. He was like a bear shot by a tranquilizer gun; there was nothing you could do to stop the heavy descent.

I curled up against him and closed my eyes, too, but I couldn't sleep, not even after the walking and travelling. I extracted myself from the cocoon of a bed and took the keys. I didn't bother leaving a note—Daniel looked like he'd be out of it for a while.

Paris was a good city for being in love, but it was also a good city for being alone. It was a good city to long for someone in: outside the hotel, I felt a fondness for Daniel upstairs. It was a chilly afternoon and I put my hands in the pockets of my jacket, picked a direction and walked. I didn't stray far from the hotel, but I meandered through the streets, looked at the window displays and found another nearby bakery that looked perfect for a morning pastry. I ended up on a busier street, lined with restaurants. I walked by a row of them and tried to figure out which one was least catered to tourists, but there was English on every menu, so I picked the closest. It was dark, and the host at the front addressed me in French, which made me feel proud of myself, like I'd dressed properly, but my French was rusty, and after I requested a table for one, he spoke to me in English.

My meal came quickly, a poached egg sitting precariously on a bed of white frisée, sprinkled liberally with dark, salty cubes of lardons, everything coated in a shiny vinaigrette dressing. A glass of white wine. I jiggled the egg with my fork and the yolk gushed into the salad. I swirled it around, the yolk, the vinaigrette. I drank the wine, and it made me sleepy, and the thought of Daniel's warm body at the hotel was more and more appealing.

The problem came when it was time to pay. I looked in my purse, and my wallet wasn't there. I'd put it in my carry-on bag on the airplane along with our passports, but when we arrived in Paris I'd switched to the prettier purse packed in my suitcase. Daniel had paid for the sandwich, so I hadn't noticed that I'd forgotten to transfer my wallet. I opened every pocket hoping to find cash, even if Canadian bills would've been useless. I had a small agenda, a digital camera, a scarf, lip gloss, the keys to the hotel. No money, no identification, no cellphone, nothing useful. After putting the contents of my purse on the table and then back, I signalled to my waiter. He raised his eyebrows at me expectantly.

"This is embarrassing," I said.

"Pardon me?"

"I flew in today—a few hours ago, actually—and I left my wallet in my hotel room."

"So how will you pay?"

"I can go back and get my wallet. My hotel isn't far; I'll

come back right away."

He looked at me skeptically, as if he heard this story all the time.

"I promise," I said.

He glanced at the bowl in front me crusted with dried yolk and glistening oil. My empty wineglass. "I'll wait for your return."

"Thank you," I said. "Thank you so much. My name is Anna. I'll be back in a few minutes."

My tiredness hit me hard and combined with the adrenaline rush of the situation, I felt woozy and flaky, like a tourist, a loud one, and shrill. I left the restaurant quickly and hurried down the streets, retraced my steps back to the hotel. I climbed the stairs for the third time in four hours and my thighs were burning.

When I opened the door, Daniel was awake, watching a French talk show on a television I hadn't noticed earlier. I knew he couldn't understand what they were talking about.

"I was worried you'd left me," he said. "In Paris, how humiliating!"

"Have you seen my wallet?" I asked.

"I haven't moved since you last saw me."

I went to my suitcase, dumped out my carry-on and found it tangled up in a sweater. "I just skipped out on a bill. I have to go back and pay."

"Now?"

"I left the restaurant without paying!" My eyes stung with tears. Was I going to cry? Recently, bursting into tears had become a habit. I'd been amazed by Zoe's sudden tears when she was a child. One minute she would be giggling, and then I would blink and her face would be transformed, streaked with tears, her nose bright red and runny. "What happened?" I would ask. "I don't know," she'd wail, "I just feel sad." Zoe was sad about so many things. Dogs tied to poles while their owners shopped inside stores. How I threw out old clothes ("I'll miss them," she sniffed, as if they were good friends). Niko would ask me what I was doing to her to make her so upset, but also realized that it was beyond us, that Zoe shed enough tears for the entire family.

I felt ridiculous, sitting there on the bed with Daniel, still self-conscious about creating a scene at the stupid restaurant.

"Are you…okay?" he asked.

"Yes." My cheeks felt hot.

"Lie down, get some sleep. You can pay later. Hell, don't pay at all. They let you leave. I'm assuming you didn't order the champagne and oysters."

"No," I said, determined to make it right. Daniel was always the logical one, and I often butted against his logic. "I'm going to pay now. Do you want to come with me?"

"Only if you promise me you won't cry about it."

"I'm embarrassed, that's all." He was teasing me, and it bothered me as much as the waiter's tone. "It's cute; I never see you like this." He hauled himself out of bed and stretched. "Don't worry about it. Really." He came over and hugged me, and I chose to believe him. "Let's go."

NIKO

At Maria and Spiro's apartment I met their pet turtle, Bouboulina, and it was that turtle that sparked everything good and everything wrong with my move back to Greece. Bouboulina was a red-eared slider, a gift from Maria's brother to their daughter, Valia, twenty-five years earlier. Valia had initially named the turtle Dimitri after her best friend. It was uninspired, but she was so adamant about it that no one questioned whether it was gender appropriate. Life with Dimitri was uneventful, until five years later, when the family woke up and discovered a small egg floating in the corner of the aquarium. Dimitri, it turned out, was a she. By then Valia was no longer friends with the original Dimitri and had been heartbroken by *other* Dimitris, so instead of logically switching from Dimitri to Dimitra, made the change more extreme. Laskarina Bouboulina was a heroine of the Greek War of Independence, an icon of freedom, and Valia was learning about her in school. Dimitri was therefore rechristened according to her history lessons. Valia moved away when she got older, but Bouboulina remained in Maria and Spiro's care in the same apartment. She never laid another egg.

When I saw her she was sitting in a red plastic bowl on the counter, gobs of dried shrimp floating on the surface of the water. She opened her mouth slowly, soundlessly, and swallowed.

"Are we having that for dinner?" I asked.

Maria swatted me on the back. "No! She's family."

"I'm afraid to see how you treat your guests."

"She's happy," she said.

After dinner Maria showed me Bouboulina's real home, an aquarium in Valia's old bedroom, as Spartan as my balcony, no neon-coloured plastic toys, no large rocks, no frills. It was an aquarium in the strictest sense of the word: a rectangular glass cube filled with water. The cleaning pump had stopped working, which was why they dumped her into the plastic bowl in the kitchen at feeding time. Bouboulina was constantly submerged unless she extended her neck to raise her head into the air.

"She doesn't mind living like that?" I asked. Perhaps turtles didn't need entertainment, but the aquarium looked cruelly devoid of existential distraction.

"She's over twenty-five-years old," Maria told me. "It can't be that bad for her. She walks around the apartment a lot, too."

Before leaving I caught a final glimpse of the plastic pail, and for the next few days I couldn't get the image out of my head. I didn't care much for animals, never grew up with pets and didn't understand the attachment people in North America had to them. Pets hadn't been popular when I was growing up. Restaurant owners would leave leftover food for stray cats or dogs, the occasional lonely old woman would keep a bowl of food out on the street for whatever needy animal happened to pass by, and sometimes one had a dog at their country home, but that was the extent of it. To me, pets created chaos in their owners' lives, cost money and then died when you'd grown attached to them.

I think I cared about Bouboulina's plight because it made

me think of Zoe. Like most girls her age, she loved animals, every single one of them. She would've doted on the turtle, asked to hold it, feed it. She wanted a cat and we wouldn't even let her have a hamster.

There was something simultaneously wise and cute about Bouboulina, the way she solemnly chomped on her dried shrimp and blinked at me. Now would be a good time to let Zoe have a pet, a distraction from the upheaval of me leaving, and I told myself to mention it to Anna the next time we talked. Anna would accuse me of giving in to Zoe's wishes when I wasn't around to deal with the consequences, but I would suggest it anyway. For Zoe.

Bouboulina also made me think of my mother because she'd written about her, the real human being, not the turtle. Like my father, my mother was also a writer. A poet. While I can't judge my parents on literary merits, my mother was the more successful poet. Her work appeared in magazines and she even published a book. The final product, *The Solitary Woman*, was elegant, and I was sincerely impressed when she handed me a copy. I'd come home from school and before I took off my shoes or put down my bag, she'd pressed the book into my hands. More than proud, I was relieved that I finally had legitimate proof that my mother had created something real. Magazines and newspapers were one thing, but everyone knew that a book was more official. Around the same time, my father worked at a newspaper and wrote book reviews. He was paid poorly, but the job was steady and he truly enjoyed it. Those years were the happiest of my childhood.

The Solitary Woman had a textured off-white cover with a navy-blue pencil-scratched sketch of a woman. The paper inside was smooth and thick. The book was short, but respectable, and I was proud when people told me that it was good. The only source of embarrassment was its title, which prompted friends of mine to ask if my parents were planning on getting divorced. I didn't answer those questions.

One of the poems in *The Solitary Woman* was about Laskarina Bouboulina. I'd also learned about her in school, and her name was found on various city streets in Athens, including one near the apartment in Kypseli. She'd even spent a significant portion of her life, and then later died, on the island of Spetses, where my father's family was from, so I was well-versed in her life.

Bouboulina was born in a prison in Constantinople in 1771. Her father had been imprisoned during a failed Greek independence revolution against the Turkish occupation, and one day, when her mother was visiting him in jail, Laskarina joined them. What a way to enter the world!

The way you're born must have an influence on the rest of your life, the way they say that what you do on New Year's Eve will affect your upcoming year. I was born at my grandmother's house, an angry squelching mass that turned yellow and thin and wouldn't drink his mother's milk, and had to be rushed to the hospital a few days later so they could diagnose what was wrong. Unsatisfied at home from the very beginning, my mother used to say.

Zoe was born quickly and cleanly at a hospital in Toronto, and she was red-faced and tight-lipped for a good minute before her first cry burst forth, loud and piercing, right in my ear. The rest of her childhood followed the same pattern: she would pause and mull things over, and then cry and cry and cry if she didn't understand. I'm sure Anna's birth was easy and secret, and her father probably didn't see her until she was wiped clean, just a sweet-smelling new-born with translucent skin and pinkish veins. She was bald until she was three years old. Anna as a baby—the most innocent thing I could imagine.

Bouboulina, like her father, took up the cause of Greek independence. According to the historian Filimon, *against her, the unmanly were ashamed and the brave stepped back*. She sailed ships, built ships, captained ships. She was exiled to Russia, but returned. She was the only woman directly involved in the underground revolution and bought arms and ammunition with her own money. She had not one, but two husbands die at the hand of pirates.

I hadn't thought about Bouboulina or my mother's poetry much in Toronto, but I remembered the first line of my mother's poem:

Forget the pirates and ignore the waves,
Adjust your scarf and carry on.
We're watching.

After that first dinner, Maria and Spiro invited me over at least once a week, and if I was too busy, Maria would give me plates of food to eat by myself. More often than not I was busy. I started work at Calypso and quickly learned that there were problems, real, significant ones. At first I chalked it up to nerves. During those first weeks, I worked later than anyone else in the small office, took the bus home, and if I didn't have any of Maria's food, I would eat the last tiropita on the rack in Elly and Thomas's bakery before falling into bed, exhausted.

Work distracted me from feeling lonely, though. I must have anticipated it given how hard I'd tried hard to convince Anna to accompany me.

"Why don't you come?" I asked her so many times. "You and Zoe, just for a year."

"Zoe's almost a teenager; she doesn't want to move to an entirely different country. And what would I say to my boss? He can't hold my position for an entire year."

"Quit! Get a new job when you come back. We'll make it work."

"But I love my job."

"That much?" I didn't understand how anything could compare with the adventure I was proposing. I was convinced she and Zoe would like Athens. Our relocated family would be happier, more tanned, and then we would return to Canada a few years later, closer than ever. We'd talked about it when Zoe was younger, how we should try out life somewhere else, even just temporarily, and I was surprised that she was now so vehemently against it.

"If you want to go, go, but there will be consequences."

Anna would drop threats like that during our discussions without clarifying exactly what she meant by "consequences." It wasn't until I had my flight booked that she sat me down and told me that if I was really going to go, she wanted a divorce.

There are certain things that shouldn't come as a shock, and the lead up toward a divorce is one of them, but I was still taken aback. She could've been bluffing, but it seemed too risky to assume. I was nervous enough to call Jimmy to delay my arrival. It turned out there was still some paperwork to put in place, so my delay didn't matter. For once I appreciated Greek bureaucracy. My current boss allowed me to continue working with them for a few more months, as well. I told Anna that I wasn't going, but I'd simply pushed my start date back. We just needed more time to sort through the details together.

Christmas was the last time we were truly happy as a family. Anna didn't know I was still planning on leaving and was relaxed and even sweet with me. It snowed straight through dinner, and after the big meal, I craved physical activity, so I went outside to shovel the driveway. With the cold air brushing against my cheeks, I felt like a man doing his job, like a logger in some forest. And then Zoe came out too, her body wrapped in neon waterproof layers, pinks and greens, the brightest creature in the white night. She grinned at me and I saw her crooked teeth. She was going to get braces to straighten them while I was away, but now they looked cute, reminders that she was still a girl. She grabbed a shovel to help me, and the two of us pushed the snow around until the driveway was clear except for the soft velvet sheen that had continued to fall while we worked. Back inside I was flooded with warmth again, and Zoe was running around and chattering loudly about something, and Anna was reading a book, her feet up on the couch.

A household, when it works so harmoniously, is a living thing, a thriving organism. I wondered why I wanted to take it apart. It was perhaps an immature thing to do, to leave, like a child ripping the legs off a spider to see what would happen to it. As a boy I'd once cut the tail off a lizard. It was one of the small, flesh-coloured and practically transparent lizards you see scurrying along walls. They mean good luck if you find them in your house. I wanted to catch it, so I chased it behind a flowerpot and when I lifted up the pot, it ran underneath. I lowered it, and as the lizard tried to escape, its tail got caught, just snapped right off. I don't know if the lizard lived or not—it just ran away—and I was too scared to get a closer look at its discarded tail.

When I confessed to Anna that I really was going to leave, that I had a flight lined up already, she didn't bring up divorce again. She didn't even get exceptionally angry. I prepared myself for something to happen, but time passed and nothing was stopping me. Anna and I didn't talk about our relationship, and while avoidance wasn't the best course of action on either of our parts, I didn't question it. We talked instead about bank accounts and taxes and long-distance plans, vacation time and doctors' appointments. Even Zoe acted as if she was at peace with my decision. She had friends whose parents went on extended business trips; it wasn't so uncommon.

A few days before I left, Zoe returned from her swim-team practice and came to my office in the basement. Her hair was still wet.

"You're really leaving on Saturday?" she asked. I nodded. She stood next to me. "How often will you call?"

We'd already discussed this, but with this question she didn't sound young and scared, she just sounded rational, like an adult, like the way Anna and I had discussed how she could reach me if there was an emergency. I could hear Anna's tone of voice in hers, calm and measured, and for a moment I thought about cancelling my trip. That I would miss the progression of Zoe into adolescence was terrifying. My contract with Calypso was technically only for a year, but a lot could change in twelve months, especially with a child. A teenager.

Despite my eagerness to take the job at Calypso, to pick up the loose ends of the business created by my family, I would still get bad feelings, little shudders of fear, like a ghost passing through me. But then they would leave and I would continue with my plans. I'd left my home before, and I could leave again. And most importantly: I could return.

I didn't understand people who wanted to settle in one spot and remain there until the day they died. I had a co-worker who was patiently counting down the years until his retirement so that, instead of weekends, he could spend entire weeks, months even, at his cottage up north, sitting on the porch, reading a newspaper or going fishing, but mostly sitting. Sitting until he died, and then he could lie in a coffin forever. I wanted to move around more than that. Weren't my ancestors sailors? They were always in motion.

Even with turbulence, I made it to Athens. My marriage was weakened, but it was still intact, and I would miss my daughter, but at least she was learning that it was okay to do things for yourself, that in the end you're the one in control of your life. I wanted Zoe to know these things even more than I wanted to leave.

ZOE

Although he'd broken up with me, I kept returning to Hugo's apartment. He never seemed thrilled to see me, but didn't turn me away or take back the key he'd given me, either. One night I arrived just as he was leaving to see his friends. I stayed, but when the sun rose and he still wasn't back, I walked around and packed up whatever belonged to me.

I left with three grocery bags of assorted items—some clothes, a few notebooks. I still had the two stones he'd given me in the park and I also had a wooden box he'd bought for me from a junk shop on Ontario Street that smelled like incense and weed when I opened it.

Susie was in our room in her pyjamas and she rolled her eyes when she saw me slink in holding so much stuff. When I started crying, she softened. I'd forgotten the way people treat you when something bad has happened: tentatively, like you're contagious, like they might catch your heart-break if they inhale too deeply or touch you accidentally.

"What are you going to do now?" she asked, as if it wasn't an option to return permanently to our shared room.

"I don't know," I said. "I think I need some time alone. I might go home for a few days. Or somewhere else."

Before moving, I'd had wanderlust. My mother had offered to pay for a graduation trip, but I'd declined so that I could spend the summer with Emily and our boyfriends. We broke up with them almost immediately and simultaneously, and by then it was too late to plan a trip. Montreal had been a good starting destination, though. Meeting Hugo had been like a voyage, too, a tunnel to a new land. Now that I'd been banished, I wasn't ready to return to real life.

"Go for it." Susie was dating one of the guys we'd gotten drunk with back in September, and I knew she wanted me out of our room longer. I didn't feel like going to Toronto, though. I wasn't ready to think about what I wanted to keep, what had to be thrown out. What about all of my father's things that we'd never gotten rid of—did Mom intend on moving them to Daniel's condo or to a storage unit?

My father used to tell me that when he was growing up, he couldn't wait to get the hell out of Greece. He said it started in the little apartment he lived in with his parents. Even without siblings, the place was tiny, eight hundred square feet stuffed with the three of them, not one spare inch of extra space.

He picked the practical way of escape: academia. He did well in school and started doing better when he pinned down what was at stake. He got into the best engineering program in Athens, and his success there was used to fuel applications for post-graduate work in the United States. He accepted the first scholarship he was offered and boarded a plane for America. The problem was that when he finished school, he wanted to move again. He thought he would settle down permanently in Toronto, but then years later he started missing Greece, and when an excuse arose to return, he couldn't refuse.

Sometimes I try to connect parts of myself to specific family members. I have my mother's nose and brown, wavy hair, which came from her mother. I got my father's parents' writing genes. When I'm restless, I don't know how it can come from anyone else but my father, and after talking to Susie, all I could think about was leaving Montreal, just for a while.

I thought about visiting Emily in Toronto without telling my mom. She'd stayed for school, although we'd fallen out of touch while I was dating Hugo. When it came time to tell her that he'd dumped me, I realized that the lack of communication had been my fault. She'd suggested visiting Montreal a few times, but I'd been cagey about it. Where would she have stayed? With me at Hugo's? I deflected the questions even though I'd walk around the city and narrate it to her in my head. During those months we hardly talked. When I visited at Christmas, we were distant with each other, even in person. I'd brought over one of Hugo's smaller paintings to show her, as if it was a stand-in for him.

"Cool," she'd said, and left it at that.

After Hugo broke up with me, I got panicky at the thought of not having her around either. I waited before telling her what had happened, because I knew that if she didn't respond or care, I deserved that reaction.

Emily and I had been best friends since we were eleven years old, a time when these declarations were made public. It had been decreed in Monica Johnstone's notebook, who spent recess stomping around school grounds and recording the social hierarchy of our classroom. Prettiest, funniest, ugliest—nothing was off limits.

"Who's your best friend?" she asked us one day, holding the notebook. She directed her question to Emily first. Emily swallowed and looked down. It was a terrifying moment. I knew I would've picked her, but I wasn't sure if she would reciprocate.

"Zoe."

Monica wrote it down. "Zoe, do you agree?"

I nodded. There were five of us standing together and so one girl was left out. She cried—the humiliation was even worse than being picked last in gym class—and our teacher ended up confiscating Monica's notebook and giving us all a lecture while the tattletale sunk low in her chair, mortified and best-friendless. But the act of Monica taking census was irreversible, and from then on, Emily and I naturally paired off.

She was supposed to move to Montreal with me. We'd made a pact when we started high school. It was almost the year 2000 and we'd told each other that if the world didn't end at midnight on New Year's Eve the way everyone was worried it would, we'd move to a different city together when we graduated. Of course it didn't end, so over the years we considered Paris, New York City, San Francisco, but when I went to Montreal with my mother one weekend and walked through its small streets, listened to the Québécois accents, saw bottles of wine and beer for sale in the corner stores, I suggested it to Emily. We could have fun there. It was, practically speaking, more doable than, say, London. She agreed.

When she told me she wasn't coming, we were in her backyard drinking vodka spiked orange juice.

"What?" I asked. "We had a pact!"

"My parents can't afford out-of-province tuition, and if I stay here they'll help me pay for school. I really wanted to move with you. I thought I could work it out, but I can't."

"I feel sick," I said.

"Me too."

We were both pathetic, Emily sad that she had to stay, me terrified at the prospect of starting out on my own. A tear fell down my cheek and left a thick, slimy trace, like a slug inching across a leaf.

At home my mother knocked on the bathroom door when she heard me retching into the toilet. I didn't open it, but I stood outside her bedroom afterwards. "Emily isn't coming with me to Montreal."

"It's good to do things alone," Mom said gently, and got up to pour me a glass of water.

My default mode was to do things alone. I was an only child, I had a small family. I didn't mind—I was accustomed to it, good at it, better than most people—but what would happen if I didn't make an effort to reach out? Would I always be alone? It was frightening, this proximity to an abyss of solitude. So, after sending Emily an e-mail that explained what had happened with Hugo, I was relieved when she responded not just by writing me back, but calling.

"Ugh," she said when I answered the phone after the first ring. "His paintings are awful."

"I know." I wiped away a few tears. With that we were back to talking every day, even if it was just sending the other a one-word text message. She kept trying to convince me to visit Toronto, that it would be good enough for whatever restlessness I had, but I wasn't quite ready.

I went to Hugo's one more time, my last-ditch effort to make him change his mind. The sex wasn't very good, and he fell asleep immediately afterwards. When he slept, he'd curl into a ball, the smallest shape he could make, and I'd reach over and hold him. It was most effective if I just smothered him with my body, slipping my arms and legs into the floppy loops of his limbs, the way you're supposed to warm a person with hypothermia. Skin on skin.

I loved the feeling of his breathing beneath me, a steady, comforting whoosh.

That night I climbed on top of his sleeping body, and his hair got caught in my mouth, and instead of disturbing our position, I blew it away, working the hairs out slowly with my tongue. I wanted to say something like, "You're the first person I ever loved," but I didn't, and even if I had, I imagined the words would've gotten jumbled up in his curls or shot haphazardly into the black depths of the bedroom.

Our relationship hadn't even spanned the length of an entire winter, but I was weighted down by a feeling of love even if it was over, like I was shrouded in a thin, lacy veil. Hugo's apartment was in a building that was more than a hundred years old, and when I first started staying there, I would lie awake at night and listen to the erratic banging in the pipes or creaks in the settling floorboards. The sounds made me think of poltergeists or restless spirits, and at first I was afraid, but then, eventually, I relaxed. I had nothing to be afraid of. This bloom of courage didn't come from Hugo, but at first, and for a while afterwards, I thought it had.

ANNA

Daniel and I rarely travelled together. His vacation time was usually spent with the girls, and I had never been comfortable leaving Zoe alone for very long. We also enjoyed being at home. I learned this about myself years ago, when Niko suggested that we move to Greece. Some people jumped at the opportunity to move abroad, and I always thought I was one of those people, until I had the chance and refused. A trip like I was taking with Daniel, five days, was perfect. Enough to feel removed, but not too removed.

After all the paranoia of his dreaded jet lag, we woke up early the next morning, ready to take on the city. We had ambitious plans, including lunch reservations and dinner, too. Soon after he had bought the plane tickets, all we could talk about was the food we would eat in France. One night at his place, I'd forgotten I was supposed to bring over dinner. Instead of going out, he pulled out everything he had in his fridge and we ate it like a picnic spread out on the coffee table. A hunk of salty blue cheese smeared on crackers, cucumber sliced thin and shocked into crispness by a bowl of ice water, four eggs scrambled and eaten while they were still wet, sprinkled with cracked black pepper, the meal even better with the knowledge we'd soon be on vacation together. Daniel took out his laptop and we looked up restaurants we wanted to try. I volunteered to make reservations so that I could practice my French, but when I called, I spoke in English.

Our first stop was the Musée d'Orsay because I knew our attention span for art would only last while we were fully caffeinated. The Louvre was too big, and although I was interested in the Pompidou, I wanted to see big, sumptuous paintings, not modern art.

Daniel's phone was in my purse, and when it rang, we jumped. He answered in case something was wrong, but it was just Stephanie, chirpy and wanting to chat.

I wandered into the next room, which had Gustave Courbet's *L'Origine du monde* on display. It was a close-up oil painting of a woman's creamy stomach and vagina and thighs, her legs spread apart just enough that you could almost see inside her. People flocked around this painting, half-embarrassed, half-indifferent.

Walking around museums reminded me that I wasn't sure how to look at art. I didn't study paintings for very long and when I did I viewed them within the context of my own life and then moved on to the next. Was that wrong? I knew I should consider them in the grand scheme of things—the political and social contexts, the lineage. Sometimes something is important only because of what immediately preceded or proceeded it. When I'd been to Paris in my twenties, I'd tried harder to be serious, and even sometimes wrote down my thoughts about certain paintings or recording names and dates to research later.

Daniel found me and handed back the phone. "Interesting angle," he said, and nodded to the painting. I didn't say anything. "Why are you so stressed out?"

"I'm not."

He squeezed my shoulders. "You're all stiff."

I stopped, breathed. Sunlight beamed in through the windows, and I reminded myself that everything was beautiful, not just the art.

"It's nice that Steph called," I said.

"You should call Zoe. Let her know you got here in one piece."

"I've tried a few times already, but she didn't answer. She's still mad at me about the house, I think."

"It wasn't her decision to make. She didn't co-sign the mortgage."

"I don't even have a place for us to live yet," I said. "I didn't think it through very well."

"She's not living with you anymore. And you can live with me for as long as you want. There's space for her when she visits."

"I know."

"I think you're overreacting."

"Maybe."

After the d'Orsay we stopped at a bakery, and I waited outside while Daniel ordered. I pulled out the phone to call Zoe. It rang and went to her voice mail again. I left a message. *Tu me manques*, I said. A phrase I remembered: *I miss you*.

Daniel emerged carrying two small boxes. "You already had a croissant today, so I got you something better."

We sat down on a bench and I opened mine. Inside there was a mille feuille, its chocolate and vanilla top hardened into a perfect sugar gloss. I pressed a plastic fork into it and it split into layers of puff pastry and cream and custard. He had such a sweet tooth, Daniel, and although I would've preferred another croissant, I didn't complain.

"You're going to Paris?" Zoe had asked when I told her about Daniel's surprise. "That's romantic. What a good boyfriend."

"Oh, Zoe," I'd said, strangely bashful. I don't know why it made me uncomfortable when she referred to Daniel as my boyfriend—it was as if she was more mature about the situation than I was. I preferred not to label it at all, even after all these years.

Zoe had met Daniel much earlier than I'd met Stephanie and Kelly. I was more reluctant to meet them, but I did want Zoe to know Daniel. When he arranged for me to meet his girls, I met Stephanie first because when I got to his apartment she'd been there all day, sick. Kelly was still at school.

"Hi," she said from a fort of blankets on the couch, her voice soft.

"Hi," I said back. I wanted to lean over and feel her forehead, but it was too motherly a move too soon. "I'm sorry you're not feeling well." I didn't mind that she was subdued for our first meeting—I was worried that she would be hostile, and at least this way she was preoccupied. Kelly, on the other hand, was more aloof. She let herself into Daniel's condo, dropped her bags at the door, kicked off her shoes.

"Oh, hey," she said abruptly when she saw me perched on the other end of the couch, next to Kelly's blankets.

Daniel was in the kitchen, finishing dinner. He came out. "This is Anna," he said.

"I know," Kelly said. "Obviously."

"Kelly," Daniel said.

I laughed. "It is pretty obvious."

He shook his head at us, and I followed him into the kitchen to help finish dinner. Shortly afterwards Stephanie came in as well, trailed by Kelly. The three of them peeked at the pot of tomato sauce on the stove and I opened the fridge to pour us cold glasses of water.

Daniel and I met the year Niko decided to go back to Greece. We worked for the same mining company, although we'd actually gone to high school together. I'd followed my father's lead and studied geology, and Daniel had landed at the same company via a background in engineering. After a few departmental shuffles, we'd ended up in the same one and met at a baby shower for a mutual co-worker. Someone had reserved a private room at a restaurant for lunch, and Daniel and I sat across from each other.

"You look familiar," he said to me first. After some digging we made the connection that we'd grown up in the same area, graduated at the same time and, finally, yes, we'd gone to the same high school. We threw out names of people we used to know. He'd kept in better touch with his friends, even with his high school girlfriend. He didn't know my best friends and I hadn't spoken to them in years, either. I never understood people who clung to high school, who had the same friends for years and then decades. It hadn't appealed to me, and something I'd loved about Niko was how our histories never overlapped, that our lives coincided at a precise point.

I remembered Daniel the way you remember someone you see in passing every day for four years and then never see again—hazily, hardly. After we'd met again, I regretted throwing out my high school yearbooks, or else I would have looked him up and tried to decipher his senior-year message.

We started speaking more frequently at work, taking coffee breaks together, and had a standing Friday lunch date. It was on the subway coming home, a few months later, that I acknowledged to myself that I thought of him too often. I thought of him during the day and sometimes, fleetingly, at night. I hoped to see him, and in the morning I would walk by his office and if he wasn't there I would be disappointed.

Before anything happened, he bought me a doughnut and left it for me to find after a meeting. Hawaiian, multi-coloured sprinkles and synthetically sweet, a flavour I thought only children ate. I took a bite, left it on my desk for the rest of the afternoon, and the dye from the sprinkles stained the napkin beneath it. Red and green and blue, a tiny, bright watercolour.

We avoided speaking of our spouses or children when we were together since we had so many other, more pleasant things to talk about. I often thought about Daniel's wife, though, what she was like, if she was nice or funny or difficult. Niko and I had missed the office Christmas party, so I didn't get the chance to meet her. She looked pretty in the pictures I'd seen, but I thought he deserved someone prettier. It was such an immature thing to think, and then, even worse, I hoped he thought I was pretty. I wasn't even sure why I thought about him so much, other than that we made each other laugh and I liked being around him more than other men I worked with. I was out of practice, though, with flirting, with crushes.

The first time we saw each other outside of working hours was at a grocery store on a Saturday morning in the produce aisle. We were both alone. We talked for a few minutes, and then went on with our own shopping, and whenever we'd catch a glimpse of the other person across an aisle, we'd wave. It was goofy. We met again when it came time to pay, and then went out to the parking lot together, our shopping carts rattling side by side on the uneven asphalt.

"Do you want to go for coffee?" he asked.

"You have two cartons of ice cream," I said, nodding to his bags. "Will they survive?"

"Maybe. They're not for me, so I don't really care."

The grocery store was in a small strip mall with a bowling alley and a psychic, but there was also a Tim Hortons. Daniel ordered a doughnut with his coffee (chocolate dip, not Hawaiian), and we talked for an hour while his ice cream melted into a sticky puddle in his trunk. When we were finished, he walked with me to my car, leaned over and kissed me, and then we returned to our families at home.

It was easy for Daniel and me to start our relationship. We slipped into it. Our kiss was awkward at first, but we pushed past it. Then we slept together and that was good, too.

He gave me presents. Little, sentimental things. I kept a heart-shaped rock he found on the beach at Lake Ontario on my desk at work. There was a pair of black crotchless underwear that he gave me as a joke, but were thrilling when I wore them. I also had a vintage silver bracelet, a series of interlocking charms in the shape of cherubs. It was pretty, but not really my style, although I'd sometimes wear it since it made him happy.

On the drive home after our first kiss, I was embarrassed how it had happened in a strip-mall parking lot, our breath sour with bad coffee, like we were teenagers who didn't have anywhere else to go. Or, more accurately, suburban adults who weren't sure how to sort out the logistics of having an affair. I didn't feel as guilty, though, not even when I saw Niko at home. I left the car in the garage and asked him to carry in the groceries. He didn't complain, he just got up and brought them in and didn't even ask why I'd taken so long.

I can make this work, I thought to myself. I didn't think of what Daniel and I were doing as an affair, per se. Nothing had really happened and it would take more than a single kiss to disrupt the ballast of two marriages and three children between us. I was sure I could somehow skew things in our favour. Not forever, but for a while.

My relationship with Niko also began because of groceries. Who needs bars when there are grocery stores on every block, some open twenty-four hours? The lights are harsh, too; you know exactly what you're getting into and could probably glean more personal information from a shopping basket than you could over a few drinks.

I was living in an apartment building on Spadina Road, north of Bloor, where there were more trees and, if you walked in the side streets, houses that I'd wanted to live in one day. I loved my little apartment, even if it was always so hot I'd have to leave the balcony door open for air circulation, and despite a group of pigeons that kept trying to roost in the corner of the balcony.

Niko had moved from Athens to Boston to go to school, and when he'd finished his degree he'd decided to stay, first working in Philadelphia and then immigrating to Canada, where he worked in a small town in Quebec until he got a job in Toronto. He'd lived on the Danforth for a year until moving to the same building I lived in, which was closer to his office. Having lived in only three different places in my entire life, two of them with my parents and all within Ontario, I was impressed by his wanderings.

We were in the lobby checking our mail. We smiled at each other and he asked if I had a recommendation for a good, cheap place to buy groceries in the neighbourhood.

"I'm heading there right now," I said. "You can come with me."

We walked to the store together. Afterwards he invited me to his apartment for a drink, and then that evening we went out for dinner. When we returned, we went to my overheated place, and the next morning he didn't leave for a very long time, and then a year later we were married. For better or for worse.

I rarely thought of those early days of meeting Daniel or Niko, because they were painful in a way. Too much raw emotion, all big feeling, not tempered and smoothed out by time and experience. I don't know if gut instincts are as reliable as people say they are, because my intuition told me to ignore Daniel and pursue Niko, and neither was right, although I suppose if I hadn't pursued Niko, my life would've been completely different, and that's impossible to conceive as well.

NIKO

On a particularly discouraging day at Calypso, I realized there wasn't any point in staying late, came home early and called George to ask about the lease to the apartment.

"How does it work exactly?" I asked. "Am I locked in?"

"You're planning on leaving us already?"

"Just out of curiosity. I might need to find a bigger place if Anna and Zoe move to Athens." I said it as if it were a real possibility instead of me just looking for a way to flee.

"There are always ways to make it work," he said, and I felt a little better.

It didn't take a finance expert to deduce that Calypso's cash flow was moving in the wrong direction. Basic math: too much money spent, not enough earned. The company could limp along for a while, but it was dying a slow death, no matter how much Jimmy and Christos rummaged up new business and conjured new plans. They were savvy, but they were also running low on new ideas.

Even though I'd been buoyed by my return to Athens, as the days progressed, pangs of regret washed over me in bigger and bigger waves. I talked to Anna and Zoe and pretended otherwise. My life outside the office was structured around our calls. On weekdays they called when they got home from work and school, around eleven or midnight for me, and on the weekends I would call in the afternoon and talk to them in their early morning. My conversations with

Anna were superficial and tense, but I still needed them, or at least relied on them. There was a comfort in the frequency. I would usually spend more time talking to Zoe, who surprised me with the things she would reveal about her life.

"We're learning how to weld in shop class," she told me one day.

"You're...welding?"

"I haven't tried it yet, but I will next week."

"What are you making?"

"A signpost. Today I bent pieces of metal around a pole. Next week I weld them together, then the week after that, I spray-paint it black or silver."

"That sounds fun."

"I'm nervous," she said. "We have to wear these special aprons and a mask. And our teacher taught us *A before O or up you will go.*"

"What does that mean?"

"You have to turn the acetylene in the torch before the oxygen or else it will explode! I'm afraid I'll turn on the O before the A."

"You won't, I'm sure of it. But why are you studying this in school?"

"You didn't?"

"I've never welded in my life."

My conversations with Zoe were always tangential and rambling. We discussed the details of her everyday life, her latest school projects or her swim team, as if I was still there. Sometimes I wished I'd just brought Zoe to Greece with me. She would've loved Athens, walking through the maze of streets. There were stray cats on every corner, and she could've picked out her favourites. She could've learned Greek, gone to an English expat school, made new friends.

The force with which I missed her alternately astonished and frightened me. I tried to ignore it, and would wait for the phone to ring instead, talk to her about her day, and then would go to bed immediately before whatever I felt developed into sadness.

When I was especially restless in Athens, I walked. I walked from the apartment to the centre of the city and back and around. I followed sidewalks, and when the sidewalks ended abruptly, which they did, often, I walked in the streets, moving aside to let cars pass by. Athens, for all its ugliness and brashness, had an invigorating spark. At night I would stroll down a nearby pedestrian street and there would be so many people out, even on weekdays. Children hyper and running, older women gossiping, teenagers smoking cigarette after cigarette at bars and coffee shops.

On one of my evening walks, I passed a storefront I knew from my childhood, the place where my mother had always purchased my school shoes. I'd hated going with her and never understood why she insisted on dragging me along when she wouldn't listen to my opinions anyway. It had now been converted into a store called Pet Corner, inexplicably in English. There were a few cages in the front window, all rabbits. Maybe they knew something about turtles? I'd been thinking about poor Bouboulina living in an empty aquarium, barely able to keep her head above water. The real Bouboulina had sacrificed everything for the sake of her country, and I didn't believe she would be happy with the turtle's living conditions. So I entered the store.

The woman by the cash register had the blank facial expression I often saw on shopkeepers forced to maintain vigil at their stores. At the bakery beside my apartment, for instance, Elly and Thomas worked every day except Sunday, from early morning until eighty-thirty or nine at night. The smell of baking bread wafted up to my apartment when the sun rose, before I got out of bed. Elly spent her days sitting on a small stool by the shelves, waiting for customers. Sometimes she would disappear into the back, where Thomas manned the oven, but the door-chime would summon her immediately. Elly was cheerful or feisty, depending on her mood and particular history with the customer. Yianni from the first floor bought his bread from them even if he didn't trust them enough to have a key to the lobby, but they didn't make any pretence of liking each other. Elly liked me, though, and always gave me large loaves that went stale before I finished them. I would catch a glimpse of her through the front window when the store was empty. Whatever welcoming smile she might've given me if I'd entered was gone, replaced with something devoid of emotion. She didn't look angry or even bored, just completely neutral, a mask hiding something deeper. Until I moved back I'd forgotten about that kind of drudgery. It existed in North America, too, but my proximity to it had changed. The immigrants I knew in Toronto were like me—we had assimilated and were successful. If there was trouble, it was hidden and we weren't constrained to a single job until we died.

The woman at the cash register at Pet Corner was named Larissa, but I didn't know that at the time, nor did I know that our conversation would be the first in a long string of conversations. I nodded at her and walked toward the back of the store, where there was a row of aquariums. Because the shop was so dim, the water had an otherworldly fluorescent tinge to it. The aquariums were stocked with fish.

"Can I help you?" Larissa asked. I could tell by her accent

that she wasn't Greek. Albanian, perhaps, or Bulgarian. She looked like she was in her early thirties. Her hair was dyed a coppery reddish colour.

"Do you know anything about turtles?"

"Not very much, but I can try to answer your question."

"My neighbour has one and she keeps it immersed in water all the time. Is that bad?"

"What kind of turtle is it?"

"I don't know," I said. "It's about this big." I held my hands apart in the approximate length of Bouboulina's shell, the size of my palm.

"I need to know what kind it is. Some spend most of their lives underwater, but for others it can be fatal."

"She's twenty-five years old."

"He's probably fine then."

"She," I corrected. Larissa smiled, although it was more like a smirk. "How long has this store been open?"

"Five years."

"Do you own it?"

Again, that smirk. "No."

"I used to buy shoes here."

"From a pet store?"

"When it used to be a shoe store. More than five years ago."

I walked around as if I knew what I was looking for. The rabbits at the front were trying to drink from a drip bottle, and their paws scrabbled frantically against their cage.

"Is there something I can buy for the turtle?" I asked.

"It won't hurt to give her something to climb. You can use any rock."

"What if I want to buy one?" I wasn't in the mood to hunt for the right kind, the right size. I wanted to get something in a box and hand it over to Spiro and Maria.

"I can order something for you, if you really want it."

I wrote my phone number on a slip of paper and handed it over. I would have the rock or stand or whatever it was that turtle owners put in their tanks shortly. I didn't ask how much it cost, and I left the store feeling as if I'd finally done something that would make someone happy.

One day after work, the phone rang earlier than usual, but I still expected it to be Anna or Zoe. Instead it was the owner of Pet Corner. The order for Bouboulina's rock had arrived.

"I've been trying to reach you all week," he said, almost gasping, I realized, from anger.

"I was at work."

"You don't have an answering machine?"

"I just moved in. I don't have one yet."

"It's completely irresponsible for you not to have an answering machine. What if there was an emergency? Next time give a number where you can actually be reached. You placed an order with me at my store."

"I didn't even pay for whatever it is I ordered," I said to him. "I have no obligation toward you. I can go to a garden and get a rock for free. You're wasting your time."

He swore at me and hung up, and for a few minutes I fumed. And then I laughed. I'd enjoyed yelling at him, just as he'd probably enjoyed yelling at me.

I'd planned on eating whatever leftovers I had in the kitchen for dinner (bread and tomatoes), but our exchange had riled me up and I went out to buy souvlaki. I sat on a bench in a nearby square and ate while watching a group of boys play soccer. I used to play in the same area. We didn't have grassy parks in the city, but we had these squares, expanses of concrete that were big enough for us to run around in and kick a ball. We weren't afraid of tripping and skinning our knees.

On work nights I had less time to walk around aimlessly, so I took advantage of being out and awake to wander the neighbourhood. I turned a corner and found myself not far from the pet store, and then, for fun, decided to visit. I could debate with the owner in person. I would buy the rock for Bouboulina anyway. Maria had given me so much food since I'd moved next door; I wanted to thank her.

The store was closed, but when I peeked through the glass, I saw someone at the back. It was Larissa. I knocked and she looked over and shook her head. I knocked again and she unlocked the door. She didn't recognize me.

"I just wanted to pick up an order," I said. "I talked to your boss—he said it arrived."

"What did you order?"

"The rock? For the turtle. Can I just buy it now? It's for a friend, not me."

Larissa let me in. "I heard your conversation. He told me to return it, but if you want to buy it, it's yours."

"Where is he?"

"He lives upstairs. He went to bed. He's not that bad, but he was in a bad mood today."

She handed over my order. It was an acrylic simulation of a rock, unnaturally and uniformly peach-coloured and perfectly flat at the bottom so it could sit neatly in an aquarium. We stood around the cash register for a few more minutes and talked, both of us seemingly starved for conversation.

The owner was an old man, widowed. Larissa took care of the shop, cleaned it and made him meals, too. She was Albanian and lived in an apartment nearby with her sister and brother-in-law. She'd been in Athens for the past five years and had lucked out in getting the job at the pet store. Her sister cleaned for one of the owner's friends, and had recommended Larissa. She started off cleaning and cooking for him, and the job morphed into her taking care of the store as well. She liked animals, and her father had been a vet for farm animals outside Tirana. She considered it fortunate that she could work in the pet store.

"Where are you from?" she asked, and I wondered if my accent had changed that much since I left. "No, you sound Greek, but you said you just returned. Where have you been?"

"Does it matter?" I asked, trying to flirt. "I'm here with you now." She blinked. "Canada," I said, stupidly. For the first time since we'd met, she seemed impressed.

There are times when you live your life first-hand, like a newborn absorbing their surroundings soundlessly, effortlessly, without realizing what they're doing. Then there are times when you feel removed, like you're watching yourself in a movie. That night I watched myself walk home, holding a bag from Pet Corner, my brain humming like a tuning fork.

I presented the rock to Maria and Spiro the following evening, and the three of us crowded around the aquarium, plunked it down and waited for Bouboulina's reaction, to see her climb on it and bask. She shuffled to the side, away from our splashing.

"You paid for this?" Spiro asked.

Bouboulina remained in the water, her heavy-lidded eyes scanning our faces, unamused, but at least her potential refuge was now in place.

I visited Larissa at the pet store again a few days later. I bought a fish this time, yellow-and-black-striped and shaped like an arrowhead. She put it in a small globe-shaped aquarium.

"A gift for one of your children?" she asked as she rang it up.

"No."

"Your wife?"

"For me. My family is still in Canada."

"You must miss them. What are you going to name the fish?"

"I'm not sure yet. It doesn't come with one?"

"You'll have to pay attention to its personality."

At home, I put the aquarium on my desk beside the phone and tapped some food into the bowl. The fish swam around, and came up quickly. Four days later I came home from work and found it floating at the top, dead. I walked back to the pet store.

"The fish died," I said to Larissa. "I didn't even get the chance to name it."

"Already? What did you do?"

"Nothing. I fed it every day. This morning it was swimming around and looked perfectly healthy."

"Fish don't live very long. It's good you didn't name him—you would've gotten too attached."

"They usually live at least a week. I think you sold me a defective fish."

"We don't give warranties on animals. Sorry. Are you sure you didn't kill it?"

"You can come over and see for yourself."

I liked the feeling of meeting someone new, a woman. At work I was with men all day and at home the woman I saw most was Maria. I started taking more evening walks and dropping by the pet store. It wasn't unusual to talk to shop owners and build up a relationship of sorts, and I wasn't going to let the fact that I didn't actually own a pet stop me.

Our first conversations were mainly about the store. The

owner had started bringing rabbits up to his apartment and he let them hop around the entire place. Larissa now had to clean up their droppings under tables, chairs, in his bed. She tried to sell the rabbits to anyone who set foot in the store.

One evening I passed by as she was cleaning up. I knocked and she let me in. "Why don't you join me for a walk when you're done?" I asked.

She hesitated for a second. "Wait a few minutes."

While she finished sweeping, I stood outside and looked at the rabbits. There were three of them, nestled in wood chips, their backs rising and falling with their breath. I tried to remember if there had been more the day before. That's what Zoe could get, a rabbit, cuddlier than a turtle, but still small.

Larissa covered the cages with a sheet and then came out of the store and locked the door. "So, you really want to go for a walk?"

I felt like it had been foolish of me to ask, but led the way anyway along the pedestrian street. "Do you like living in Athens?" I asked. I was thinking of Yianni and the bakery, and his contempt for Albanians. I knew many people, good people otherwise, who shared his opinions. Casual racism notwithstanding, on a purely practical level, with all of its bureaucracy, Athens was a difficult city to live in.

Larissa nodded her head. "Are you happy to be back?"

"Enough," I said.

I stopped at a store and bought us ice cream. It seemed like a good move, like there was something silly but gallant about it. Or was it too fatherly? Why did I even care? We sat on a bench.

"Why are you doing this?" Larissa asked. "You come by all the time. You must have other friends."

"A few."

"Why isn't your family with you?"

"My wife didn't want to come."

"Why not?"

"I'm not sure."

We ate in silence. To an observer, my attraction to Larissa must have appeared purely sexual, but it was more than that. I knew how hard Athens was for outsiders, and now that I was back, I related to that fact and wanted to share it with someone. Larissa and I could have seen Athens from similar perspectives.

When she finished her ice cream, Larissa got up first.

"I have to go. My sister will wonder what's taking me so long."

I leaned over and kissed her on both cheeks. The custom, an innocent parting. She wouldn't let me accompany her home, so I watched her walk away.

I'd assumed I would slip easily back into life in Athens, but after so many years abroad, I had too many North American customs ingrained in me. The people I saw most—my neighbours, my co-workers at Calypso—welcomed me with open arms and treated me as if I were one of them, but every so often they would say something or do something and I would realize how different we were, how much I'd changed.

I'd been an outsider many times. Before I moved to the U.S., I read a book a friend had recommended to me about the customs of American youth, everything from dating to grooming habits. You read these books and you know they're essentially useless, but you do it anyway and hope to get some tips. Eventually I got used to the place I lived in, learned the tricks, accepted the differences, but it took time. It was tiring having to go through the routine again, this time in a place I was supposed to be familiar with.

When I was growing up, Kypseli was homogeneously Greek and relatively affluent, so our apartment was considered to be in a good area despite my father's precarious employment situation. Demographics started changing around the time I left. Most of the nicer homes were torn down and replaced with the same kind of five-storey buildings I was currently living in, and well-to-do people migrated to the suburbs, which resulted in a large number of vacant apartments and, over time, an increased number of immigrants. In the nineties, when thousands of Albanians fled because of trouble in their country, Kypseli became a hub for cheap lodging in Athens. There were Russians and Poles too, and even Africans. When I'd moved to the United States, my lab partner was the first black person I'd ever spoken to.

I saw some women, but the immigrants were overwhelmingly men. I wondered what it was like for them to come here. Who cooked for them. My own meals were a pathetic blend of sliced vegetables, takeout from various restaurants and whatever food Maria passed on to me, usually full meals during the week and desserts on the weekend. Sometimes I made eggs, and when I was really lazy I would just crack some in a bowl and stick it directly into the microwave. I'd watch the eggs rise into impressive-looking bubbles and then quickly deflate and cook into a rubbery mass.

Once, when I was too busy to do laundry, I bought socks from one of the young African men selling goods along the side of the street near my bus stop. There was always a row of them, their white blankets covered with a mish-mash of things: knock-off designer sunglasses, underwear, posters (the Virgin Mary next to Michael Jackson next to kittens perched on a wall on a Cycladic island). I picked up a six-pack of fake Calvin Klein socks. While the man counted out my change, I asked him if he had a wife. He knew enough Greek to understand me.

"Yes," he said. "But she's not here."

"Is she going to come one day?"

He shrugged.

"I'm not sure if mine will come either. I'm from Canada."

He gave me my change, not eager for conversation. I knew I shouldn't identify with him. I had money, options. I was Greek; I had a Canadian passport, too. I could leave if I wanted to, easy. I still wanted to talk more, ask him how he coped, how long he'd been here and if things had gotten easier, even though I wasn't sure if, for him, they ever really would.

Larissa had more in common with him, but when I talked to her, I forgot there was any difference between us. Because our interactions were limited, the realities of daily life kept mostly at bay, it was easy to believe we were on the same wavelength, that I'd found a kindred spirit.

ZOE

A few weeks passed, and I still found myself in Montreal. Susie, unsure of what to make of me, would leave our room in the morning, and then text from a safe distance away. *Are you sure you're okay?*

I didn't know how to answer her because I wasn't sure myself. I was lonely, mostly. Whenever I got into one of these moods, I thought of my grandmother's book. My father's parents had both been writers, and when I took a shine to writing as a kid, he said that I must have gotten my poetry-writing gene from them. My grandfather had been the weak link in a family chain of seafaring men, an artist instead of a mariner, and instead of working in his family's shipping business, was a journalist. My grandmother wrote, too, and even published a book, a slim volume of poetry called *The Solitary Woman*.

It was one of the few things my father kept from his childhood that he thought could survive a move abroad. Growing up, I'd flip through it, not understanding its contents but reassured by its existence. I paid particular attention to the book after my father died, and somehow decided that it was about my mother, even though it was written years before my parents had even met. I viewed my mother as a solitary woman, though. She wasn't bogged down by it, but strengthened, and I was sure that my grandmother's book assigned her the kind of bravery and beauty that only comes with poetry.

I'd once tried to translate parts of the book with a Greek-English dictionary. The only poems I could vaguely understand were the shortest ones. Little wisps.

Under three pine trees
near a country path
beside a rock and resting on
grey dust
I planted a story of solitude.

I'd brought the book with me to Montreal, and after breaking up with Hugo, I pulled it out. I wondered if I'd gotten it wrong: maybe I was the solitary woman—could that be possible? I suppose, if anyone, the solitary woman had to be my grandmother, since she was the one who wrote the poems. I went to the bookstore to buy a Greek dictionary; now would be a good time to try translating it again.

The first thing I did was flip through the book looking for proper nouns, like my father's name. I never found it. There were other names scattered throughout, though, mainly towns or islands. One in particular intrigued me. Phonetically, *grey*, but spelled with a bizarre combination of a's and e's: *Graeae*.

I looked it up and learned that it wasn't a place, but a thing. A trio. The Graeae were three sea nymphs who'd been born with prematurely grey hair and shared one eye. They were most known for their role in the myth of Perseus and Medusa, when Perseus held their eye hostage until they confessed Medusa's whereabouts so that he could track her down and lop off her head.

My grandmother's poem transposed the idea of the Graeae to her family. One of the first lines I translated was:

My family, the Graeae
a single eye, three hearts.

I liked the idea of three people sharing an eye, that link
between them. Who was I linked to now? My father wasn't
around anymore to be the third person with me and my
mother, and I wasn't anywhere close to starting a trio with
anyone else. Still, it made me feel more solid. I sometimes
felt like my family was insignificant compared with the rest
of the world, people who had accrued presence over time
and could flaunt it at their Christmas and Thanksgiving
gatherings. We didn't have that clout, except now I had this
poem from my grandmother and even though it wasn't
about my mother, my father and I, it was close.

I'd go to a café or to the library with my laptop and work on
translating the poems. Occasionally I tried to write my own
poetry, too, or do some school work. If all three activities
frustrated me, which happened often, I went online.

When I was still having a hard time dealing with my
father, Mom enrolled me in a support group for teens with
dead parents. I met them reluctantly once a week at a com-
munity centre downtown in a room that looked out onto
a track. Often I'd tune out of the discussion and stare at
the joggers going around in endless circles. Maybe jogging
would be more helpful for me than the support group.

When the session started, we introduced ourselves by
talking about how our parent had died. Most of the deaths
were medical—cancer or heart attacks, for instance—but occasionally there were accidental cases, like my father's. The
existence of death in our lives, the premature violence of it,
bonded us, and framed our relationships within the context

of personal misfortune. Our common thread was bad luck.

I met the first boy I ever kissed, Jonathan, here. His mother had died from breast cancer. We both took the same route home, but I would hang back until he left, since I was too raw after these sessions to talk. One evening he asked me to walk with him, and it felt rude to turn him down. In the end we didn't speak much anyway.

The next time, when we were close to the station, he took my hand. I didn't pull it away. He led me to a bench in Spadina station, the section where the streetcars enter at the junction between the two subway lines. People walked by us in a steady stream, Asian grandmothers with bags of produce from Chinatown, university students with frayed backpacks, business people on their way home from work, and no one stopped to sit on the bench with us. Jonathan leaned over and kissed me hard on the lips. I later figured out that I should lean into him, too, that the kiss was better if I actively participated in it.

Week after week, we would make out on the same bench. During the support group, it was unspoken that anything we said was directed toward the other. When he said, "You guys are the only people who understand what I'm going through," I knew he meant only me, and when I nodded my head vigorously in agreement, he blushed. We never said these things to each other in private; we just kissed.

And then one day I woke up and didn't want to talk about my father anymore. The make-out sessions with Jonathan weren't incentive enough, and I didn't even go back to say goodbye. Later I wondered if I'd hurt his feelings by leaving, but by then it was too late to find him and apologize. I didn't even know his last name.

Other than learning how to kiss, the other thing I took

away from these sessions was a list of online resources that I found crumpled at the bottom of my bag. I logged in to the suggested chat group out of curiosity. It was empty, but there were other rooms, and after floating from subject to subject I settled into one about music. I chatted to people not about death, but everything else. Life, I guess. They were around my age, scattered across Canada and the United States, and our conversations would last late into the night.

The desktop computer was in the basement, and at first Mom didn't know how long I was chatting until the bill came and she saw how severely I'd exceeded our monthly bandwidth allocation. Up until then we hardly used the Internet, so the spike was surprising. She humoured it at first.

I tried to get Emily interested, but she was half-hearted and not nearly as excited by these immediate new friends as I was. When I logged in, I felt a rush from the anticipation of who would be there. Sometimes there would be a crowd of people, like a party, and sometimes there would be only two of us. Those one-on-one conversations were oddly intimate. Once you were stripped down to the words typed on a screen, all kinds of secrets and feelings came out. It didn't matter that we didn't know each other in real life or that I was sitting there in my pyjamas—we were connected.

My attachment to my online friends waxed and waned depending on what was happening in my real life. When I got a boyfriend, I logged in less frequently, and by the time I graduated and moved to Montreal, I'd stopped completely. It happened all the time: someone who would be there every single day for a month straight would disappear, return to wherever they came from and you would never hear from them again. It was my turn. Now and then I would log in to see if I recognized anyone's name, but the others had also moved on, replaced by a new cast that I didn't bother getting to know.

There was, however, one person I kept in touch with. Peter lived in New Jersey, and I'd had a crush on him at first, particularly after he'd sent me some blurry digital photos of him playing guitar. We e-mailed each other—the kinds of e-mails that weren't necessarily directed to the other person, but an excuse to pour everything out, to write paragraphs knowing that someone else was reading them.

One afternoon after giving up on both a school assignment and my grandmother's poems, I sent Peter an e-mail. He'd written me eight months earlier, but I hadn't responded.

> *Hellooooo. Do you remember me? I live in Montreal now and it's winter. Are you there?*

He wrote back right away.

> *Hey, stranger. I'm here, but by "here" I don't mean Montreal.*

We started exchanging longer e-mails, rambling ones, and I loved writing mine a little more than reading his.

> *You keep telling me you need to get away,* he wrote one day. *I'm not sure if that's a hint, but why don't you come my way? We can meet in NYC and you can stay with me if you want. I know it's kind of lame that I live with my mom, but she won't mind. I'm not busy these days— come today if you want.*

I'd known Peter online for a few years and the words, the e-mails, they amounted to something even if we hadn't met in person or even spoken on the phone. I forwarded his e-mail to Emily.

Go. Just give me his phone number and address in case he's a psychopath.

I didn't think he was, and anyway, I'd gone to Hugo's apartment less than an hour after meeting him and even though it had ended badly, it wasn't because he was dangerous.

I calculated how much money I could spend on a short trip. Dating Hugo had ended up being economical: when we went out he'd paid for both of us because he'd stockpiled so much from his parents. I could actually afford to go to New York for a few days. I could meet Peter and write poems or work on my grandmother's translation and then come back and continue going to class and getting on with my life. A reset.

I checked the bus schedule online. Why not just leave right away? I didn't wait for Susie to come back to tell her what I was doing; I just left a note. Mom was leaving for a trip to Paris with Daniel so I didn't bother telling her either. I threw clothes into a backpack and then before leaving I wrote Peter.

Okay, I'm going to New York. I'm going to leave now before I change my mind—I hope that's okay with you? See you soon! Byeeee.

In my rush I'd misread the bus schedule and arrived at the station two hours early. My phone wasn't charged, and Hugo's was the only number I had memorized in Montreal, so I called him from a pay phone to pass the time. He answered after three rings.

"Hey," I said.

"Hi." There was a pause. "How are you doing?"

His voice on the phone made my heart lurch around my chest and my stomach and legs and arms, too. We hadn't spoken since I'd taken my things from his apartment, which was now almost a month ago.

"I'm at the bus station." I had a hunch that he might show up if I told him what I was doing, not out of love, but out of curiosity, and he did. He came a half-hour later, his hair stuffed into a toque. Soft grey. I'd given it to him for Christmas. It was lumpy and loose, and when I held it in my hands, I felt like I was holding the discarded skin of a baby elephant.

"Why are you going to New York, exactly?" he asked.

"I'm meeting a friend."

He sat down next to me and put his hand on my knee. "I missed you."

We started making out in the station, wet sloppy kisses that were a little desperate, a little gross. When it came time for me to board the bus, I swung on my backpack. It was heavy and threw me off balance. My lips stung.

"You can call me whenever you want," he said.

"Thanks."

I almost stayed in Montreal and followed him back to his warm apartment. But I didn't. I got on the bus and took a window seat and even though I looked, I never saw him lope away. I thought about it, though, how his body curved over, the way he tucked in his chin and jammed his hands into his pockets. He walked like he was aerodynamic and as I thought about his walk, I wondered if anyone would ever think that way about me.

ANNA

Instead of getting lost again, Daniel and I used the map to finally figure out the most direct route to the Eiffel Tower from our hotel. The Champs de Mars was crowded with groups sitting directly on the grass or on their own blankets. We counted at least six people who posed for pictures by positioning their hands so that it looked like they were holding up the sides of the Eiffel Tower. African men sold water bottles and fake silk scarves, or, more discreetly, bottles of wine and cigarettes.

Daniel leaned back. He pulled my arm and I lay next to him, the grass slightly damp beneath me.

"This was a good idea," I said. "Paris."

"I know. I'm glad you agreed to come."

"Why wouldn't I?"

"You can be difficult."

"You're used to it by now."

We went through this routine every few months: I was the hard one, Daniel easy. Not easy as in a pushover, but he didn't get worked up over things the way I did—he wasn't stubborn. I'd say this to him as a compliment, how easygoing he was, but sometimes he was offended. "I'm not always so easy," he'd say. "If I was, we wouldn't be where we are now." I got the feeling that Daniel was excited by the complication I'd brought into his life, the way I'd been excited by the complication of meeting Niko when I was younger. There was a satisfaction in upheaval and destruction when you were the one in charge.

On the Champs de Mars, he turned over and stared at me.

"Do I have something in my teeth?"

"I was going to wait to do this, but I think I should just do it now."

"Do what?" I sat up.

"I was thinking that now would be a good time to get married." He twisted and fished something out of his pocket. A small box. "I know you don't like anything too fussy."

The ring inside was thin and delicate. It sparkled from tiny diamond chips embedded in the band. This was the second time he'd proposed to me.

"I should've waited until after dinner. Or the end of the trip. I had it planned out! I was going to ask you on our last night, on the Eiffel Tower. But we're here now and I didn't want to wait. Should I have waited? I just think it would be good for us. You can move in with me permanently or we can buy something new. We know we want to spend the rest of our lives together."

"Right."

"And we've talked about it."

"I know."

"So what do you think?"

I didn't say anything. I looked up at the sky, a swirling grey watercolour above us.

"You're killing me!" Daniel said.

"I don't want to *not* marry you."

"That's not exactly a yes."

"Didn't you say that I was difficult?" I hated myself for being cagey, but I couldn't bring myself to say yes. My lips couldn't physically form the word.

"So you'll think about it."

"Of course I will. I'm thinking about it right now."

"Thinking is overrated."

"I just need some time."

A man came by and quietly asked if we wanted to buy a bottle of wine. "Do you have any time?" Daniel asked him. He looked at his watch and replied in French.

"Merci," I said. "We don't want any wine."

"Actually, I need a drink." Daniel got up and stopped him as he walked away. He returned with a bottle. Screw-top. "I asked him if he had champagne, but it's not like we have anything to celebrate." He took a swig, no glass or cup, and handed it over. It was bad.

"So what now?" he asked.

"Did I just ruin the trip?"

"It depends. Is that a no?"

"No."

"So it's a yes."

"No. I don't know."

"Can you at least keep the ring in your purse? You didn't notice the bulge in my pants?"

I picked up the box and looked at the ring again. "It's really beautiful."

The first time Daniel proposed was a few months after Niko died. We were at a restaurant, drinking from a bottle of burgundy while we waited for our food. I'd ordered steak frites, rare.

"I wanted to do this sooner," he'd said. "But it wasn't appropriate then."

I'd looked around and hoped no one in the small room had heard what he said or my resulting gasp. "It's still not."

Daniel had blinked, closed the box. He always had bad timing when it came to proposals.

"You were about to get divorced," he'd said gently. "It's okay."

"It's not okay. I'm sorry."

Our waiter arrived with our dishes, set them down in front of us without noticing or acknowledging any tension. I don't know how we managed to get through that meal, but we did, cutting the meat and chewing and not talking. This is how we fought, in silence, but when we were in his car, he got angry.

"I know how hard things have been, but you have to move on. You were about to move on. You don't have to play the role of a widow if you don't want to. You owe it to Zoe. Otherwise tell me that it's over. You owe me that."

He was right, but I hadn't been ready to hear him say it or respond. Still, when we parted ways that night, I knew we would speak again soon.

And with time, things smoothed out. I lived in the same house; I still worked the same job. Daniel took a new job at a different company, and that made it easier, too. We kept seeing each other, and when I was ready, we stopped hiding it. Zoe met him and liked him. We spent our weekends together if he wasn't with the girls, and then during the week we would take turns, sometimes at his condo, sometimes at home. At first it was only his condo, never my home, but I relaxed about that, too. We talked about getting married lightly, not seriously, more like a smug, pleasant joke.

The proposal in Paris was nothing like the first one—it wasn't inappropriate or too soon, but it confused me anyway.

When Niko proposed to me I didn't hesitate to accept, but I'd also been so young when we met, still buzzing from the trip to Paris and my affair with Jean-François. I loved Niko right away, as soon as we met. He had wild black hair and was strong and sexy and had an accent, but he knew English well, too. On our first date he took me to a restaurant on the Danforth and ordered in Greek. We ate saganaki, the cheese fried in a blaze of flames by our table and then doused with a squeeze of lemon. The spectacle of it had been a bit campy, but it still impressed me. He bought loukoumades from a nearby bakery for dessert, fried balls of dough bathed in honey. We ate them with a shared plastic spoon, and when he kissed me I tasted traces of honey on his mouth.

A few months earlier, I'd broken up with the boyfriend I'd dated throughout university, Stephen. He thought we'd get back together once I came back from Paris and had kept calling and trying to change my mind. I almost relented, but then I met Niko and there was no going back.

My parents didn't like him. My mother was afraid he would make me move to Greece. She was thinking of our stay in Kirkland Lake, and before that, all the other small mining towns she'd had no choice to live in with my father when he'd started his career.

"Are you sure about him?" my father asked a few days after meeting Niko for the first time. I was at their house for dinner. My father had never questioned my choices of partner, not necessarily because he liked them, but because it was a topic we didn't discuss. Him saying something about Niko meant that his reservations exceeded his embarrassment over talking about personal issues with his daughter.

"What do you mean?" I looked at my mom for support, but she averted my gaze.

"He's old, isn't he?"

"Not really. He looks older because he has some grey hair."

My father cleared his throat. "And he doesn't need you for...immigration purposes?"

"Of course not! He's a Canadian citizen. He has a passport. Jesus Christ."

"Anna," Mom switched gears. "It just happened very quickly. That's all."

After we finished eating, I picked up the plates and brought them to the kitchen. Mom took her place behind the sink and I stood beside her to dry. I hated drying dishes, but did it anyway on the night I most wanted to leave. I could have gotten into my own car, driven back to my own apartment, easy.

"What does Stephen think about this?" she asked.

"He doesn't think anything about it; we don't talk."

"I'm sad that I never got to say goodbye to him properly."

"He's not dead! Call him if it makes you feel better. Invite him over to dinner. I don't care."

I left the kitchen, but still didn't leave the house. I went to my old bedroom and sat on the bed, smoothing the bedspread underneath me. It was a new comforter, floral, one I never would've chosen. Ten minutes passed, a half-hour. I went back to the kitchen and put the dishes away, and we spoke nothing more of Niko or Stephen. I kissed both my mother and father goodbye before getting back into my car and driving back downtown away from them, a warm Tupperware container of leftovers my mother had packed sitting on the passenger seat.

It's funny how things change, how certain you are of something and then how suddenly you aren't. Does it mean that you never truly felt it in the first place? I don't think of Stephen anymore. I knew my breakup with him didn't impede the progress of his life, that he got married, had three children, but for a three-month period I was afraid I was solely responsible for its outcome.

Stephen and I had spoken of our future so many times, and when it evaporated, that want for it, all that was left was a nagging tug of guilt and obligation, the ugly residue of love. If Stephen and I had gotten married, I'm sure our wedding would've been a grand affair. I'd have gone with him to his sister's, and it would have lasted an entire weekend, with the wedding rehearsal Friday, the church ceremony on Saturday afternoon, the reception late into the night, and a brunch the following morning. I would have had a different dress for each day. My parents would have come as well, and my mother would have been so impressed by the fanfare.

I didn't want a wedding like that, and when Niko and I announced our intentions, my mother didn't push it. My father asked me if I was pregnant. When Niko came over that evening—I'd told them on my own first—my parents hugged him anyway and I truly believed that the smiles on their faces were sincere.

I think they eventually saw the effect of Niko on me, or at least resigned themselves to it. It was physical. I have the pictures from those years, and I look more beautiful in them than I think I've ever looked in my life. Is that what love does to you? I was enjoying the moment; I was basking in it.

We went to City Hall and then to my parents' house for a very small reception. My mother had catered dinner, roast beef and potatoes, a salad. Wine and cake. The cake was the one thing that looked like it belonged at a more lavish wedding—three-tiered, much too large for the small group we'd assembled, perfect white icing and strewn with candied nasturtium and violet petals. The bride and groom on top of the cake weren't plastic, but heavy, like chess pieces, and had been used on my parents' wedding cake, too. Their lips were painted on in red with little black dots for the eyes, the man in a top hat and the woman in a flowing white dress.

"You're supposed to smush the cake in my face," I said to Niko.

"Smush? Like smash?"

I took my piece of cake and smeared the corner in his face. He jumped back and then laughed, took a piece and rubbed it in mine. I only ate cake that afternoon. The meat and vegetables were too heavy for what I was feeling.

Our life together was built on events like that, afternoons like that, until one day, years later, I questioned if they were adequate foundation. I still remember the sense of ceremony I felt when we cut into the cake, more permanent than whatever had been pronounced at City Hall, the crumbs sticking to our faces when we brought the forks to our mouths. Later I found frosting dried in my hair. I picked it out and wiped my hands on a discarded tea towel on the kitchen counter and then joined Niko again in the dining room, hoping to taste it again soon, the cake, that sweetness.

NIKO

After the ice-cream incident, I continued visiting Larissa at the pet store and, miraculously, she didn't push me away. She even went on more walks with me, although because she didn't want her boss, her sister or brother-in-law to see me, I would let her pick the route and we'd end up on side streets I'd forgotten about. I knew few people in the neighbourhood and didn't particularly care about their opinions.

My old friends had mostly moved to the suburbs. I'd gotten together with some of them when I'd first moved, and although it was interesting to see how everyone had turned out—who had gone bald, gotten fat, ended up married or divorced—I didn't feel the need to go out of my way to see them more often. George had also tried to introduce me to his social circle, but I'd bowed out of most of the invitations. "I'm too old for new friends," I told him.

One night when it threatened to rain, I suggested that Larissa come over to my apartment for a drink. I'd asked her casually and she'd accepted with the same kind of casualness. Once we got to the building, it occurred to me that our relationship, if it could be called a relationship, was unusual. Out in the street or in the store, it was simple, just two people walking next to each other, not even touching, and when we did, it could be deemed accidental. In the small elevator on the way up to my apartment, I was aware of our bodies, their closeness.

We sat on the balcony. The air was cool and heavy at the same time, and the clouds in the sky were backlit by the moon. All I had was beer, so I poured us each a glass and cut some baklava that Maria had given me the day before. I noticed Spiro's outline on the other side of the balcony partition. Normally he would call over and we would chat for a few minutes, but that evening he remained quiet, and I didn't say anything to him, either.

Larissa and I sat there until the rain came, and then we grabbed our drinks and went inside. I don't know how I appeared to her. Physically, I mean. There were some advantages to having lived away from Greece for so long. I looked younger than other men around my age, for instance. George was actually younger than me, but you wouldn't know it. His skin was wrinkled and rougher than mine, a by-product of living in the sun. At least Canadian winters had preserved me.

Bachelorhood was also helping me lose weight, and I had a tan from my daily commutes to the office, so all in all I looked better than I had in years. I was still noticeably older than Larissa, though. My apartment was shabby, too—the walls bare except for that icon in the bedroom. The few photos I had of Zoe and Anna were on my desk at the office since I was there more often. I never made my bed in the morning, and it was just an embarrassing messy tangle of sheets. Underwear and shirts on the floor, like a teenager.

None of that mattered. We stood in the front room looking at each other. I took her glass and placed it on the desk. During our years of marriage, I'd never been unfaithful to Anna, never even thought about it, but I wasn't concerned about her when Larissa and I kissed for the first time, when I put my arms around her and she lifted her face up to meet mine.

I usually slept with the balcony doors in the bedroom open, even if it was cold. I liked the breeze, the noises. The view when I was lying down was like a Cubist painting, all corners and angles of the surrounding buildings, rectangles of clothes hanging on lines to dry. There were always a few pairs of underwear or socks, some towels or sheets. Never anything nice or delicate, though. The nicer things were taken to the dry cleaners or dried inside so that the grimy city air wouldn't sully them. A shorter building in front of mine had a red terracotta-tiled roof, and I'd watch cats sleeping in the curve of the tiles, where they would be safe from oncoming traffic or people shooing them away. I felt invisible looking at other apartments from my bedroom, but the first thing Larissa did was close the doors so that no one would see us.

Since my bed was really two single beds pushed together, we stayed on one side and it reminded me of the first time I'd had sex in my college dorm in America. The two beds started shifting apart anyway, until there was a few inches of space between them.

Larissa didn't linger when we were finished, and I didn't ask her to stay. She got dressed, said goodnight. Shortly after she'd left, the phone rang. Canada. I didn't answer it. I'd fallen asleep through calls before; it could happen again.

That weekend, I brought Maria and Spiro some new turtle food for Bouboulina that I'd gotten at Pet Corner. "It's good for her shell," I said. "It will make it stronger."

Maria took the bag and invited me in. "How's work?" she asked. "You come home so late."

"You're paying attention to my schedule?"

"Even if you don't want to, you end up noticing things about your neighbours."

"That's why I was happy to leave Athens. There's no privacy here. In Toronto, everyone has a backyard and a fence and you have to call before visiting someone's house."

"Are you thinking about returning to Canada, then? Missing your family?" So Spiro had said something. "Anyway, I made galaktoboureko. Take some back with you." She went into the kitchen and came back with a large slice of custard and filo pastry, syrupy and still warm.

"This is my favourite, thank you."

"Not baklava?"

"My favourite after baklava."

"When your wife visits, I'll teach her how to make it."

I went back to my apartment and leaned against the counter in the kitchen and ate every bite.

I visited Larissa at the pet store the next day and the owner was there as well, even though he usually went to bed early.

"Can I help you, sir?" he asked when I came in.

"Just looking," I said.

"What are you looking for?"

Larissa was fiddling with some boxes and ignored me. I excused myself and left the shop convinced that she didn't want anything to do with me again. It was probably for the best. A relationship with her was unsustainable; it didn't make any sense.

At home, someone buzzed at the door, and through the crackle of the ancient system, I heard her voice. "I shouldn't have come," she said.

I let her in and waited for her to take the elevator up. She wrapped her arms around me first, and we went to the bedroom quickly. I was clumsy, removed from the comfortable routine I had with Anna. I kissed Larissa's breasts and she pushed my head away. I thought she was stopping me, but she wasn't, she was pushing my head lower, down her stomach, and I was embarrassed for having to be guided.

After that night, Larissa visited me regularly after she closed up the pet shop and before she went back home. I stopped going to the store as frequently. She usually left before Zoe and Anna called, but once we were still lying in bed when the phone rang. I got out of bed and answered, talked to them like any other day. While Zoe was telling me about a science project, Larissa got dressed. I gestured for her to wait, but she didn't. She didn't come over the next evening, so after work the next day I went straight to Pet Corner. There were no customers.

"How may I help you?" she asked.

"Is anything wrong?"

"No."

"I miss you."

"I think you should buy another fish."

"Larissa."

"What about a rabbit? It will live longer and it's softer and it takes up less room in your bed."

"Please. I'm sorry. I truly miss you."

We stared at each other. Her cheeks were flushed.

"I'll see you later," she said.

I wasn't sure if she'd said it to get rid of me, but she came over that night after work, and then again the next day and the next.

ZOE

The bus stopped for a break in Albany. It was early morning and my legs were cramped and I had a headache, but I took a deep breath and decided that I was okay. Not good, but not bad either. Sometimes everything got mixed up, the sadness I felt about Hugo, the sadness I felt about my father, the sadness I felt about my mother. They were all different categories of sadness that would swish together so that I couldn't distinguish one from the other.

My grandmother's poems were making me think about my father more than I had in a long time. I translated a fragment on the bus, the overhead light on until the woman next to me elbowed me and told me turn it off:

I think of you
sometimes, always
never.

From the bus depot, Albany looked empty and grey. Maybe this was what I needed first. The thought of New York City frightened me for a minute, all those cars and people and tall, tall buildings. They could wait. There are good parts of sadness, and at that moment I'd crawled into one of them, a soft cocoon of solitude and quiet.

"Can you open the luggage compartment, please?" I asked the driver. "I need my bag." He was sitting at the wheel, drinking coffee and staring out the window. "Hello?"

He didn't look at me. "Not until Port Authority."

"I don't want to go to New York City. I'm just going to get off here."

He shook his head and kept drinking. "You paid for New York."

"I'll give you twenty bucks?"

He finished his coffee and got up. "If your bag is stuck at the back, you're not getting it."

Outside he opened the luggage compartment, and since I'd been one of the last people on the bus, I saw my backpack right away. I took out a twenty-dollar bill, but he shook his head and turned around. I sat on a bench and noticed that the woman I'd been sitting with had already taken my window seat. Her big white forehead pressed against the glass, and I watched it until the bus rolled away to New York City without me.

I had no expectations for Albany, no preconceived notions, nor any way of getting my bearings. I couldn't associate a landmark with it or think of one notable thing to have ever emerged from the city. I walked in the only direction that led toward population: down a sidewalk, along a road.

I found a Holiday Inn and walked into the empty lobby. "Do you have any rooms available?" I asked.

The guy at the desk was young. His name tag read *Jonathan*, and it reminded me of my support group days, that first kiss. It was a good omen.

"Let me check." He typed things into a computer and looked up at me. "What do you want?"

"A room. For one."

"Queen? King? Smoking? Non-smoking?"

"What's the cheapest?"

"I can give you a queen for $125."

"Per night? Can I get something cheaper?"

"Are you an AAA member?"

"No."

"Any family in the military?"

"I'm Canadian, does that help?"

"Not really." He scrolled through something on his screen.

"I didn't know you could negotiate hotel prices."

"There are ways." He looked up. "Okay, I can get you a king-sized bed for $75 a night."

It was still more than I wanted to pay, but Jonathan looked so proud of the rate that I accepted it. When he found out I didn't have a credit card, he was stumped. "How can you not have a credit card?"

"I have cash; I can pay you now."

After ten more minutes of typing and exchanging money, he handed me the key to the room. "It won't be ready until two."

"What time is it now?"

"Eleven." My face must have sagged in disappointment because he leaned toward me and started speaking quietly even though no one else was around. "Listen, I know the room's clean and ready. Go, I'll take care of it."

The room was on the second floor, with a window that looked onto a parking lot and a highway. The bed was sprawling and there was a painting hanging above it, a forest landscape of green, draping trees and a dark blue river, a stark contrast to what I saw outside the window.

I lay down, and the bed was so big that I could position myself in any direction and there were still miles of plushy white bedding stretching out around me. I took off my clothes, slid underneath the sheets, and the weight of the heavy blankets was so comfortable that I slept for four hours straight, the kind of sleep that sucks you in, like a black hole or a time warp. I woke up sweaty.

In the bathroom there were a million mirrors and they all fogged up when I took a shower. I rubbed a spot dry and looked at myself reflected over and over again as I combed my hair. The steam shone in the lights like dust motes in a sunbeam.

I left my room for a walk. Jonathan was talking to someone at the front desk, so I grabbed a map and went outside. The streets were still empty—because it was a Sunday? I made my way to the only thing that looked interesting, Empire State Plaza, and when I got there, I was surprised by how vast it was. It was paved with white concrete and marble and had gigantic monoliths flanking the sides and a reflective pool running down the centre. On one side of the square, there was a structure shaped like an egg, and I got the feeling that I'd been transported to a version of the future, like I was in a science-fiction novel. This city was weird.

A group of boys were skateboarding, but I heard them before seeing them. The wheels rolling against the smooth concrete made the best scraping noise. I watched them for a few minutes, until a voice came crackling over a loudspeaker telling them to stop. I couldn't see a guard—he must have been watching from above. The kids rolled for a bit longer before hopping off their boards and lazily walking away.

I sat on a bench and looked straight ahead. It was still grey out, but it was starting to feel like spring. I'd spent so long either huddled in Hugo's apartment, the blinds open for light, rarely venturing outside, or in my own bed. At Hugo's we'd always sit on the floor, not the couch, cross-legged, knees touching, facing each other and talking. Or we'd sit side by side with our backs against the couch, and I would lean my head on his shoulder or in his lap. I never talked so much as I did with Hugo, the words just spilling out of my mouth, tumbling and rolling around. In some ways I'd been constantly trying to charm him with what I said, trying to make him laugh or feel like I understood exactly what he was feeling or saying. I'd gotten used to a certain quantity of speech, and ever since I left Montreal, my words bounced pointlessly around my head.

I said a few words out loud, just to hear my voice. I wondered if anyone would be curious about me in Albany the way Hugo was when we met, but after the skateboarders left, the plaza was empty. I pulled out my notebook and chewed on the tip of my pen.

I'd written my first poem when I was in the third grade, about snow falling. *It fell softly*, I wrote, and *sparkled like diamonds*. Not too shabby for a kid. My teacher mentioned it to my parents, and that was when my father first told me about how my grandparents used to write poetry, too. He showed me *The Solitary Woman* for the first time. I'd written the snow poem quickly, in one sitting, and I'd been satisfied with it in a way I'd never felt about anything else. I kept chasing that feeling, but none of the poems I'd written recently felt right. Words came slowly, awkwardly, or not at all, but I didn't want to leave the bench in the Empire State Plaza until I'd gotten something down on paper.

I gave up when I got too cold. There were no taxis, so I walked back to the hotel as briskly as I could. Jonathan was still at the front desk.

"Hey," he said. "How are you?"

"I'm hungry," I admitted. I'd eaten a cranberry muffin at

the bus station in Montreal and I'd had a doughnut and a bagel that morning, but I needed something more substantial. "Is there somewhere cheap to eat around here?"

"Not really, if you don't have a car," he said. "It's the weekend. Most businesses around here are closed; it's a government town."

I started heading toward the elevator, defeated, but Jonathan stopped me. "If you don't mind waiting, I can bring you somewhere."

He was wearing a white button-down shirt and his hair was cut short and I could see the ghost of a few zits on his neck and jawline. His cheeks were pink—he was embarrassed about asking.

"That would be great," I said.

"I'll call you when I'm done my shift."

Back in my room, I lay in bed with my shoes on until the phone rang. I followed him out of the hotel to the parking lot. His car was messy and he cleared a backpack off the front seat before I sat down. "Is McDonald's okay?" he asked.

Jonathan was a college student. He was attending SUNY for business and he'd worked at the hotel for the past two years. He liked it, he said. It was easy. If no one was around, he could study at the front desk. He was planning on staying in Albany when he graduated and combining his business degree with what he knew about hotels and tourism. He asked me about my plans for the future, and at first I assumed he was joking, as if I looked like the kind of person who had a good answer to that question.

At McDonald's, we sat with our trays in a corner. He'd ordered a six-pack of Chicken McNuggets in addition to his Big Mac.

"What are you doing here, anyway?" he asked.

"I'm going to New York City to visit a friend, but I felt like stopping here first."

"Where are you from?"

"Montreal."

"Cool." He dipped his fries in the McNuggets sauce and offered it to me, too. "Have you been to New York before?"

"Never."

"You'll love it."

"How do you know?"

"Everyone does."

Jonathan talked to me about the type of people who stayed at the hotel, government workers or business people who stayed in town for a few days for conferences or meetings. He could always tell which couples were having affairs. He told me about a football player he'd checked in last weekend; I didn't recognize the name, but Jonathan assured me that he'd been a nice guy who had even left a good tip for the cleaning lady, which was something people often forgot or just didn't do.

"Do you have a boyfriend?" he asked on the drive back. No other cars took the highway exit for the hotel. Downtown Albany was truly no man's land on the weekend.

"I don't. Do you? A girlfriend, I mean."

"Jill," he said. "She's at NYU. I see her on the weekends, but not so much recently. She's been really busy."

"It's almost finals."

"Yeah, I guess."

Jonathan was so nice; I hoped Jill would come back, or if she didn't, that he'd find someone nice in Albany. He was the type of boy I should fall for. I thought about what it would be like to date him, to live in the grey peacefulness of Albany and learn how to skateboard in the Empire State

Plaza, to meet minor celebrities passing through hotels—not many, but enough to build up a good repertoire of stories.

He pulled into the hotel parking lot and we both got out and stood outside.

"Thanks for the drive," I said. "And the food, and the rate."

"It was no problem, Zoe." He rubbed my shoulder when he said it. If he'd hugged me, I would've wrapped my arms around him without hesitation, and if he'd kissed me, I would've kissed him, too, even though he had a girlfriend, even though I don't think I really liked him that way.

"In case you need anything, here's my phone number. If you get bored tonight or if you want to stay in Albany, you can call." He hesitated. "I'm an idiot; I don't think I ever told you my name. I'm Bill."

"It's not Jonathan?"

He looked confused for a second. "I couldn't find my name tag this morning, so I borrowed someone else's."

"Oh," I looked at him again in the orange glow of the parking lot light, and it was funny because he didn't look like a Bill.

I took the slip of paper. This time we did hug, but it was a bit unwieldy, too much space between our bodies, and maybe I wouldn't have actually kissed him if he'd tried.

I watched Bill's car back up and he blinked his lights at me. The person working at the front desk was an older man, and he ignored me when I entered through the automatic doors. Was he the real Jonathan?

I kept Bill's number on my nightstand and felt like it radiated something good. I fell asleep easily and didn't dream of anything, or if I did, I couldn't remember when I woke up early the next morning to catch the first bus to New York City.

ANNA

After Daniel proposed, we stayed in the Champs de Mars, finishing off the bottle of wine. The phone rang. We hadn't been saying much to each other, so I was relieved to have a distraction. Zoe.

"Finally!" I said when I answered.

"Hey, Mom," she replied, less enthused. My daughter, it turned out, was in New York City.

"Is everything okay?" Daniel asked when he saw my agitation. He rubbed my calf.

I nodded my head and tried to get more details. I was worried. Zoe was old enough—we weren't even living in the same city anymore—but New York was so much bigger than Montreal, and her reason for being there, to visit a nameless friend, was flimsy, I wondered if she was lying to me.

"Keep your cellphone on," I told her. "Don't worry about how much it costs, just call me if you have to."

"How's Paris?" she asked, as if she hadn't heard.

"It's fine." I didn't say anything about the engagement ring, even though I was clutching the box in my other hand. When we hung up, I sunk back down and shook my head. "That was so strange."

Daniel and I spent the walk back to our hotel talking about Zoe. It started raining and we only had one umbrella, so even though we huddled close, our outside shoulders and backs got wet. We gave up and hailed a cab, walked up those hotel stairs, lay down in the bed. The wine had made us sleepy, and we woke up an hour before our dinner reservations at a Michelin-starred restaurant.

"My head," Daniel said, and buried his head in the pillow.

"We don't have to go."

"What else are we going to do? The meal will be our punishment for that bottle of wine."

We got up and headed out into the night together, the ring still in its box at the bottom of my purse.

Despite the question of Daniel's second proposal looming over our vacation, we focused on other things, like settling into Paris's circadian rhythm. It quickly felt like we'd only driven a few hours away, not flown across an ocean. We'd wake up early in the morning, but not too early, and we didn't have any problems sleeping at night. What neither of us had anticipated, however, was how easy it would be to sleep. Even if we didn't think we were tired, we fell asleep immediately when the lights went off, as if the sheets were coated in a sedative. This meant that two and a half days into our vacation, after Daniel's proposal, after more than a few indulgent meals accompanied by bottles of wine *and* after strolls through narrow Parisian side streets and over bridges crossing the Seine, we had not made love once.

"Are you saving yourself for our wedding night?" Daniel asked that night when, after we pulled the covers up and kissed, I turned over and closed my eyes. "I'm afraid of how long I'll have to wait."

"There's too much pressure to have amazing sex here," I said, half-muffled. "Let's brag about how much we slept instead. How long it lasted."

"It was intense. The sleeping."

"Exactly."

"I'll be perfectly happy with just plain sex, though," Daniel said after a moment. "It doesn't have to be amazing."

We kissed again, but my head was heavy, my limbs, too, and we didn't get much further.

Sometimes I forgot that Daniel and I didn't have to hide our relationship anymore. There was no reason to. He'd actually separated from, and then later divorced, his wife early on, even before Niko left for Greece. Neither were happy, and Daniel suspected she was also having an affair. Occasionally his wife would take the girls to her parents' house and he'd be alone for a week or two, and maybe if I hadn't been around, this pattern would've continued or gotten better. Instead they did what Niko and I should've done: discussed it like mature adults and moved on. When he told me, I didn't really believe it would happen, and every time we said goodbye, I told myself that it might be forever. And then he had a lawyer, and there were meetings, and he rented an apartment and he was no longer married.

With Niko abroad, we were practically single again. There was no pressure, we said, to be with each other. Except I hadn't really ended my marriage. Divorce should've come up the minute Niko talked about returning to Greece, and it definitely should've come up as soon as I started seeing Daniel. If I'd been honest with myself, it should've come up even earlier. It was shocking how easy it was to let something so big slide. I was sure about my feelings, and then I'd talk to Niko and say the opposite of what I felt. I'd done the bare minimum to stave off the inevitability of having to choose. Was my true self really so avoidant?

Daniel still thought that I'd begun divorce proceedings with Niko. I let him think that only formalities had been left, some papers to be signed, logistics worked out. Niko had packed up his clothes and moved to Greece, after all, and I'd stayed behind with no intentions of joining him. Forthcoming divorce wasn't a stretch. But when Niko left, I hadn't said anything serious to him about getting divorced. I'd brought it up once, quickly, and then never again. Instead I'd get angry and tried to stop him from leaving, but then I watched him leave, kissed him goodbye and spoke to him on the phone every few days.

I couldn't quite believe that Niko had actually left. He'd spoken seldomly of his family's shipping business until suddenly it seemed like the most important thing in the world to him.

He'd told me about KML when we first started dating, and the first time I went to Greece, he introduced me to his uncle, who was still running it. He brought it up again only after his mother died. I didn't even realize Calypso was still operating. He thought he could rescue it somehow, whip it into shape. He looked boyishly dreamy when he talked about it, and I didn't automatically discard the idea. I pictured moving our family to Athens, and a Mediterranean lifestyle, all that fish and white wine and olive oil, could be good for us.

The more seriously Niko mapped out his plan, the more I poked holes in it. What would I do in Athens? I couldn't speak Greek, I knew no one there. I enjoyed my job. Zoe was at such a transitional stage in her life, early adolescence, that an unnecessary move would be difficult. And there was no guarantee that Niko would actually like the job. Along the way Daniel popped into the picture and I didn't want to leave him, either. I didn't mention that part.

"I'm not going," I said to Niko one night. "To Athens. I think it's a bad idea. You don't know anything about boats."

"Ships," he corrected. He took a different approach. "I'll go by myself then. I'll start with a year, and we can take turns visiting each other. You can decide if you want to come later."

He said "year" as if it was a weekend, as if we had an unlimited amount of them left in our lives. We were in bed and I looked at him until my eyes adjusted to the darkness. His chest heaved up and down evenly and his face was relaxed. It wasn't unusual for couples to separate temporarily for work purposes.

"Are you joking?" I asked.

"I think it's a good plan."

Going away would have been the perfect opportunity for us to make a clean break or for me to just continue on with my affair with Daniel without worrying about getting caught. Still, I thought that if I could convince Niko to stay, our marriage would be fine. I would end things with Daniel, and life would continue as was.

Three days later, Niko said, a tiny, gentle surrender, "Okay, I'll stay."

We kept volleying back and forth—Niko going off on his own and scheming a way to return to Athens, me expressing dismay and waiting to see how he'd react. The fax machine in his office in the basement rang in the middle of the night—incoming from Greece. I'd look at the shiny pieces of paper, but they were in Greek and I couldn't decipher them.

Every time Niko said, "I'm not going," I would be flooded with a relief that I think I confused with love, like I'd somehow won. Maybe it was just competition. I didn't want to be left behind for something else, even if that something wasn't a person. It was hypocritical of me to think this while having an affair with Daniel, but I couldn't stop myself. And in the end, Niko left. I guess I lost.

Fundamentally I believed that events had to stack up one on top of the other until they reached a climax that would then set off the next set of events. Life was a gigantic seismographic chart, a buildup of deep, underground rumbles that eventually got too big and bubbled to the surface. I was testing how much I could keep buried until it started to show. It turned out I could withstand a lot.

NIKO

At Calypso, of the two brothers, I knew Jimmy best. Christos spent most of his time at a vacation house in Mykonos, and if he was in Athens, he'd learned the term *working from home* and would say it with gusto, in English. He specialized in taking people out for dinner—clients, port authorities, other friends in the shipping industry. Jimmy thrived on the day-to-day work and liked the way people looked at him when he walked into the office. He often showed up late, but at least he would show up. Jimmy liked that I'd lived in North America for so long. He'd ask me for advice or would take me out for lunch near the port for seafood to talk about work or women or money.

"What do you know about sailing?" he asked me at one of our first lunches.

As a child, I'd thought working in shipping was the most interesting career a person could have. I imagined myself as a sailor, and having access to the rest of the world was alluring. Alexander would bring me to the ships when they were in port, and they were each their own separate empires. I would clutch the salt-crusted bars and peer down to the sea below, flat green, garbage floating on the surface, and tried to guess how deep the water must be away from the port. Deep and cold and clean. The middle of the ocean must be like outer space, I thought, but even better because you still got sunlight.

My father tried to dissuade any romance I held about voyaging at sea. "You're trapped on the ship," he told me. "You have nowhere to go, and if you're sick, you can't go to the hospital, and if you die, they just throw you overboard. You're away from your family and friends for months and you're surrounded only by men. You don't want that life."

"Alexander likes it," I would protest.

"Alexander doesn't go anywhere—he's not a sailor. He just likes being in charge."

Being trapped on a ship didn't seem much worse than being trapped in my current life. We had little money and few options. I might as well have been stuck at sea for all the places I could afford to go, and at least a ship was bigger than our apartment.

As I grew older, I looked beyond the sea and decided I'd have more opportunities if I just moved elsewhere. On a ship you were bound to return home, so I figured the best course of action would be to shift my definition of it. I studied and got a scholarship and stipend to do my master's degree in the United States. When the acceptance letter arrived, my father sat across from me and asked, "Is this what you want?"

"Yes."

"What is it exactly you want again?"

"To leave."

"Well, congratulations."

Now that I was working the job of my childhood fantasy, the big ships that Calypso specialized in, the bulk carriers, were still foreign. My job was so far removed from Calypso's daily activities that the actual shipping of goods across bodies of water was intangible, theoretical.

"I don't know much about sailing," I admitted to Jimmy.

"But your family is made up of sailors! We'll have to do something about it."

A few weeks later he invited me to his weekend home on the island of Aegina to teach me how to sail. I left on Friday evening after finishing up at the office. You could take either Flying Dolphins or regular ferries to Aegina, and I chose a ferry, even though the Flying Dolphins, boats that skim the water quickly, took less than an hour. The ferry was bigger and slower and required an additional hour of travel time, but I wanted that extra buffer. It would feel more like a trip that way. I bypassed the air-conditioned interior and walked to the outer deck. Only a scattering of people were outside, and I couldn't hear their conversations over the din of the engine.

The water churned white behind the ferry and a group of seagulls soared in the tail wind, occasionally diving head-first for food. Athens dissolved into a mirage in the distance, its edges smoothed by a band of smog. Away from port, the air smelled fresher. Saltier. I studied the hazy outlines of islands, soft, gentle rolls of land, as the sun set.

I didn't have an address for Jimmy, but the taxi driver knew which house I meant when I described it to him. We wound through empty, dark roads until we arrived at a blaze of light where Jimmy, his family and some friends were sitting outside, eating dinner. I heard their laughter before I saw them. The group of us were going to go sailing first thing in the morning.

I slept in a small guest house with heavy stone walls and cold cement floors. The bathroom was in its own separate space next door, unconnected. When I woke up in the middle of the night, the darkness, silence and cold were disorienting. I went to the bathroom, but before re-enter-ing the guest house, paused outside. I hadn't experienced such profound silence since arriving in Athens, and it echoed in my ears. The darkness looked like a void I could fall into forever. You don't think of darkness as having colour, but in Aegina I noticed the difference in shades: the treeline was darker than the sky. I stood there until I got three mosquito bites in a row.

Jimmy knocked on the door when the sun rose. "Wake-up call!"

It was peaceful on the boat. The winds were calm, and we sailed smoothly away from Aegina.

Up until the trip, I didn't think of Jimmy as a physically active person, but he came alive on his boat, and was happier adjusting the sails and steering than lying on deck with us. Every time he did something new—pulling the jib, tying a new knot—he'd call me over and walk me through the steps, and then make me repeat it for him. If I fumbled, he would patiently guide me through the action again.

At lunch, we swam off the boat. I was nervous, but jumped in anyway, and the freezing sea water made my muscles stiffen. I surfaced and gasped and, instead of panicking, dunked myself underwater again. It reminded me of the fact that I was alive, that I was a physical body. Being with Larissa had the same effect on me. That afternoon I sailed by myself for an hour.

"It is in your blood!" Jimmy called to me. "Look at you!"

I'd revered the water when I was younger, but stopped thinking about it as I got older. I visited the ocean a few times when I moved to North America, but those beaches were eerie to me—big stretches of sand, so much shore. The beach isn't important in Greece, just a thin strip of land to leave your belongings on. The starting point to dive into the sea. Ocean waves were rougher, too, and I remembered the shock of being dragged under by one, how swiftly it had flipped me over and made my nostrils burn with salt water.

That night, when we returned to Aegina, Jimmy guided the boat into port silently. A full moon cut a dusty yellow path before us. The moonlight was just enough to reflect the images of the surrounding boats in the shimmering water. No one spoke; what could we say to do justice to this scene? It was beautiful, but I was suddenly lonely, the only single man in the group.

Back in my apartment the next afternoon, I was restless. I called Zoe and Anna first, but got the answering machine, so returned a call to George. The last time I'd seen him I'd spent far too long complaining about the mothballs in my closet. Even though I'd tossed them out, their scent had embedded into the wood permanently and was now infecting my own clothes. I'd catch whiffs of mothballs while I was at work. He'd called to offer me a dresser from his house that they weren't using. He described it to me, but I didn't really care about decor, so accepted it without question.

After we hung up, I picked up the receiver again. Larissa had given me her phone number, but I'd never had a reason to call. I dialled slowly.

"Who is this?" A man, probably her brother-in-law, answered.

"It's…Jimmy."

He passed the phone over to Larissa. "Yes?" she asked, confused.

"It's Niko."

"Why did you say your name was Jimmy?"

"I don't know," I said, and she laughed at me. "Listen,

do you want to come over? Maria gave me another half-tray of baklava she just made, and I can't eat it alone. And I want to see you."

Even though she'd been to my apartment many times before, I was still surprised when she agreed to come over, and then arrived within the next half hour.

While Larissa and I were on the balcony, someone knocked loudly on my front door. We both jumped. I got up and looked through the peephole—it was George. Shit. I'd assumed he'd come by later in the week, not right away. I opened the door for him.

"Who let you in downstairs?" I asked. "I didn't hear you buzz."

"Hello to you, too, my cousin! I need your help." The dresser was too big to fit into the elevator so it was sitting in the lobby. While George turned to the elevator, I gestured to Larissa that I'd be back in a few minutes.

We each grabbed one side of the dresser and carried it slowly up the stairs. The trip to Aegina had left me feeling strong. George, on the other hand, started sweating immediately.

"Let's bring it straight to the bedroom," I said when we entered the apartment. I guided him so that his back was to the balcony, but the apartment was too small to hide anything, and he saw Larissa right away.

"I didn't know you had guests," he said in English with his thick Greek accent bleeding through.

"Just a friend from the neighbourhood."

"I see."

We set the dresser down. I offered him a drink and we walked to the balcony, although I could sense hesitation in both our steps. I didn't want him to meet Larissa, but it would be more suspicious to kick him out.

"This is George, my cousin," I said when we went outside. "This is Larissa."

They nodded at each other. There were only two chairs, so I ran inside to grab another, and when I came back I could tell that neither had spoken in my brief absence. I sat down between them. Larissa reached for her drink, and I realized that the shirt she was wearing, which had seemed modest at first, was not as modest when she leaned over.

George gave me the briefest of looks. He knew Anna and Zoe. When he and Katerina had visited us in Toronto before having their children, I'd given them the grand tour of the city, made sure to bring them to the CN Tower, and then took them on a day trip to Niagara Falls. Zoe came along with us. She was five years old then and just as awed as George and Katerina by the sight-seeing. At the top of the CN Tower, George had lifted her into the air and slowly lowered her toward the glass-bottomed floor of the observation deck as if he was baptizing her in the invisible waters of downtown Toronto, and she'd screamed with fear and delight.

"Have some food my neighbour made." I offered him the tray.

I did my best to get the conversation going. We talked about the baklava we were eating. We talked about the weather. I talked about my weekend in Aegina. We didn't discuss anything notable from Larissa's life. She excused herself after ten minutes, said it was getting late and that she had to go home. I got up to walk her to my door. She wasn't saying anything to me, so I followed her out of my apartment and into the elevator.

"You don't have to escort me out," she said.

"I'm sorry if that was uncomfortable. I didn't know

George was going to come over."

"It doesn't matter."

"He won't say anything."

"About what?"

"Us."

"What is there to say?"

"Come on."

"I hope he doesn't say anything to your wife, then. I'm not worried about him saying anything to anyone I know."

"I'm not ashamed of this."

"Good for you." She let herself out.

Up until that point, I'd reconciled my relationship with Larissa. It hadn't felt wrong; I hadn't felt guilty. It was just a part of my new life here in Athens, which was completely independent from my life in Canada. Nothing had changed with Anna and Zoe. I even still brought up the fact that they could come join me if they wanted to. Anna continued to brush it off.

I took the elevator back up. George was still sitting on the balcony, eating the baklava. He'd helped himself to another beer from my fridge. I grabbed one too and sat with him again.

"You told me you didn't care about making new friends," he said.

"When in Rome?"

"We're not in Rome, though."

"She's a very nice girl." I was embarrassed for calling her "girl", but it had just slipped out.

"I'm sure she is."

"I would appreciate if you didn't mention this to anyone."

"What is there to mention? Anyway, I didn't see anything out of the ordinary, did I? You were just having a drink."

"Right."

We clinked bottles and stopped talking about Larissa. He didn't mention her when he left, and didn't ask about her in the future either.

ZOE

The atmosphere of the station in Albany was the complete opposite of the bright, noisy 42nd Street Port Authority bus depot. I followed hallways and tried to make sense of the signs, and when I picked an exit, I was still confused, but at least I could breathe fresh air after hours on the bus.

I was too intimidated to deal with the subway, and after looking at a map figured I could make my way uptown toward Central Park until meeting Peter later in the afternoon. I passed Times Square and walked into the crush of tourists, some dawdling and taking pictures, others motoring through without paying attention to who they were jostling.

It's strange being in a place you've heard so much about. I'd been excited as we pulled into the station, but now I felt scattered. The city had so many people in it and everything was pushed close together, and I'd expected this blend, while completely obvious and expected, to be somehow more revelatory, life-changing.

Walking through the numbered streets calmed me down—42ND, 43RD, 44TH. I concentrated on checking them off one by one. I bought a pretzel that tasted only of salt. I got an enormous cup of coffee from a truck, wrapped my fingers around it and drank it black in big gulps.

When I made it to the edge of Central Park, my shoulders were sore from my bag and my feet were tingling from pounding the pavement. I looked up at the trees around me. Trees, buildings in the distance, even more buildings behind me. No one knew where I was, and I liked this sense of root-lessness, of being obliterated by everything around me.

My mother was now in Paris and had already left me two messages. I could tell she was worried about why I wasn't calling her back. I'd finally told her about Hugo, and even though I'd spun it as a mutual decision, I knew she was concerned about me. She answered after a few rings. The connection was staticky—were the trees in Central Park in the way? "Hello?"

"Mom? It's me."

"Zoe! I tried calling you yesterday and the day before."

"I know, sorry I didn't answer. I'm out of town, too."

"What do you mean?"

"I'm not in Montreal."

"Where are you?"

"New York City."

"New York City?"

"I'm visiting a friend."

"A friend? Who? Are you by yourself?"

"No…Emily's here's, too."

"Don't you have class? Both of you?"

"It's only for a few days. Anyway, how's Paris?"

"I'm still confused about why you're in New York."

"I just needed a break."

"You could've come home, Zoe." She took a deep breath. "I know you're sad about Hugo."

"It's not that."

"What is it then?"

"I wasn't ready to come home and start thinking about what I'd have to pack and throw out. I didn't want to go through all of Dad's things again."

"You don't have to worry about that, honey." Her voice was tight, and I briefly wondered if she was going to cry or if it was the connection or if she was just annoyed with me. "Do you have enough money?"

"Yes. Do you want me to get you anything while I'm here?"

"Like a souvenir?"

"I guess."

"No, Zoe. Don't buy me anything. Jesus."

"I'm fine, Mom. Really. I'll call again soon. Or e-mail. Enjoy your vacation; you don't have to worry about me."

After I hung up, I realized that not only had Mom been genuinely flustered on the phone, but that I'd enjoyed it. She was one of the calmest people I knew. Growing up, my father had been the one with extremes in emotions, a raging storm of anger or a jubilant pool of happiness, not many points in between. My mother, on the other hand, was subdued and understanding. She never got angry with me. I remember being a kid, crying because she wouldn't buy me a stuffed animal we'd seen at a store. "I hate you," I'd said to her, over and over, not caring who could hear me. "I know," she'd replied, rubbing my back.

Peter and I had arranged to meet on the steps of the New York Public Library behind Bryant Park. As I approached, I got nervous. I'd never met any of the people I used to chat with online, and everything that could go wrong, that I had told Emily not to be worried about—that he wasn't who he said he was or that he was but that he was also a murderer or a rapist—cycled through my head. And even if he was just a regular non-murderer, non-rapist guy, what if he had intentions other than friendship? Did I?

I spotted him first from far away. It was undeniably him. His hair was sun-bleached blond, almost white. His eyebrows and eyelashes were the same colour, and at first I couldn't see them clearly. His eyes were a pale blue, and later, when I knew him more up close, I noticed delicate traces of veins on the insides of his wrists in the same colour.

"Peter?"

"Zoe?"

We hugged, stiffly because I was wearing my backpack, which he then offered to carry. We talked to each other like we'd met before, I suppose because we had in a certain way. "Let's go inside," he said, and led me into the hushed reading room of the library, which had constellations painted on the ceilings. Afterwards we walked through Bryant Park, and the bare tree branches were studded with little buds waiting for the right moment to flower.

He brought me to a place to buy dumplings, five for a dollar, the kind with broth cooked in the dough, little portable pouches of boiling soup. We sat on tall stools and slurped at the dumplings, our plastic chopsticks clicking against the sides of our bowls.

We went to the MOMA as well. By then, the combination of endless walking and the rush of caffeine and adrenaline had made me practically delirious, so I trailed behind Peter as we made our way floor by floor, bottom up. The paintings and sculptures blended into a nonsensical swirl of random images, and nothing stuck until I got to Henri Rousseau's, *The Sleeping Gypsy*. The smooth lines of paint made me pause, and they looked slick and fresh, even though Rousseau had painted them in 1897. The painting was of a woman sprawled out in the sand, a mandolin beside her. It was nighttime and there was a full moon. A lion hovered in the background, but the woman was fast asleep, dreaming and oblivious.

I liked how calm the woman looked in the painting, and even the lion wasn't threatening in that light. It was a miracle to capture moonlight and darkness, the dusty grey of a night sky. The light at night, the way it leaked in, was so much more mysterious and ephemeral. I could write poetry about *that*. Mom had told me not to get her anything, but I stopped at the gift shop and found a postcard of it anyway.

Peter's mother was at work when we took the train back to his house. We slipped off our shoes in the quiet hallway. He gave me a Coke and something about this ritual made me feel like I was in high school again. His bedroom was messy, but not too bad, and the bed was made. There was a plant by the window and piles of CDs next to a stereo. The laptop he wrote to me from was on the desk.

We sat on the floor and leaned against the bed. He pulled a box out from under it. It contained a baggie of pot, which he offered and I declined. The box also had little toys in it and newspaper clippings, and piled on top of everything was something that looked like a doll's head.

I picked it up. "What is this?"

"A shrunken head. My dad gave it to me. He bought it in Thailand." His father was a violinist in an orchestra and was often on the road for performances. His parents were divorced.

"Is it real?" I examined the head up close. It was a monkey with dark and leathery skin and flared nostrils. The hair on its face was exquisite, whorls of tiny strands, like fingerprints but prickly. The eyebrows were perfect.

"Its head was boiled before the skull was removed and

then boiled more to shrink it down."

"God, poor monkey."

"It was already dead."

"Still." I stroked the thin traces of eyebrows, the little nose. It was almost human.

Peter had a laundry basket of folded clothes at the foot of his bed, and I peered into it. "You have a lot of T-shirts," I said, and then he opened a dresser drawer and showed me more. T-shirts in different colours. T-shirts with band names. T-shirts with pictures or logos. I picked through them and asked him to explain them to me. This type of show and tell took less energy than conversing. There was a T-shirt his father brought him from Dubrovnik and one of Boston (the city, not the band). There was a *Paris, je t'aime*, too.

"So you broke up with your boyfriend?" he asked after digging up a Montreal Expos T-shirt. "You haven't really talked about it since you e-mailed me."

Broke up. It always sounded like such a petty description when someone else said it, so normal and everyday, something that happened to scores of people around the world, one a second maybe, like there was a statistic out there if you researched hard enough. At first I'd thought that whatever had happened between me and Hugo was more than just breaking up, more powerful and soul-crushing, but as time passed, I accepted that yes, that was what had happened.

"He dumped me, actually."

"Asshole."

"Do you have a girlfriend?" I'd left so quickly that we hadn't actually straightened out many details ahead of time.

"Nah," he said. "Well, I did but we broke up a few months ago."

"Right."

I picked up his wallet. He didn't stop me from flipping through the cards inside. He looked so young in the picture on his driver's licence, even more baby-faced than he was now. I pulled out my own and showed it to him. In the picture I had short hair, a bad homemade job Emily had helped me with when I was sixteen.

"So how long are you staying here?" he asked after studying it. "I'm not rushing you or anything; I was just wondering."

I had a paper due in a week and I was behind in the class, but I hadn't bothered bringing any of my notes with me. "Just a few days," I said. "As long as you're okay with me staying with you, really."

I wasn't exactly sure what Peter did with his days. He wasn't in school—he'd told me he was taking a year off while he decided what to do.

"How are you getting home?"

"The bus."

"Do you have your ticket already?" I shook my head. "What about if I drove you?"

"Do you have a car?" I took my driver's licence back, tucked it into my wallet.

"I do. Almost, anyway. I'm sorting out the details."

"It's a long drive from here to Montreal. I'm not sure why you would want to."

"The same reason you came here—I just want to go somewhere."

"Maybe we can decide later?" I yawned. It was only nine. "I'm not usually tired this early."

"It's okay," he said. "We can talk about it tomorrow."

I stayed in the guest room next to his, and that night I dreamt I was in a skyscraper in New York City, looking down at the cars and taxis and people. All the little dots.

From far away a tidal wave approached the city, towering high above the buildings, dark blue and frothing and about to drown us all. I didn't cower as it approached; I just stood there and watched as it got closer and closer, and I never once closed my eyes or flinched.

I woke up to Peter talking to his mother, who was on her way to work. I was too cotton-mouthed from sleep to get up and introduce myself, so I waited until silence settled over the house again to creep out of bed. I took a shower and changed before saying anything to Peter. He was also fully dressed when I was ready. We were polite with each other, not very talkative, and it wasn't until we were on our way to the train station back to New York that we relaxed.

Instead of going to Manhattan, we went to the Bronx. He hadn't been kidding about the car—he'd just bought one from a friend of his named Wolf ("Wolf?" "Yes.") and was finalizing insurance, so the car was at Wolf's apartment until it came through in a day or two. It had belonged to Wolf's grandfather until he'd moved into an old-age home. Wolf had driven it for a few months, but he didn't need it in the city, so he'd sold it to Peter for next to nothing.

When we emerged from the subway station, I didn't feel like I was in the same New York City I'd been in the day before. I mean, I knew the Bronx would be different from Manhattan, but I was still surprised. The roads were wider and there were car washes everywhere.

I expected Wolf to be sleazy, but he was just a regular guy in jeans and a T-shirt. He and his girlfriend, Lucy, lived in a converted factory building. The apartment was big and the rent was relatively cheap since the area wasn't completely gentrified yet. Lucy sat on the couch and watched us while she smoked. Wolf, on the other hand, wouldn't shut up. He also kept calling Peter "Pete." Because he'd introduced himself to me as Peter, I couldn't think of him as a Pete. It was too casual, too unserious, for what I knew of him.

"Let's check out the car," Peter said, cutting Wolf off from a story he was telling us about their previous night, something involving a bottle of whisky and an attempt to scale the sides of the Brooklyn Bridge. The four of us took the industrial-sized elevator down to the ground floor.

"It's a good, solid car," Wolf said to me, as if trying to convince me of its worthiness.

Peter got in the driver's seat and Wolf sat next to him. Peter had only driven it once since buying it, and we sat there while he flicked the blinkers and the lights on and off and then turned on the radio.

"I don't remember if I told you that the air conditioner is broken," Wolf said.

"How do you know each other?" Lucy asked me while they went through their.

"Long story," Peter said before I had the chance to answer. Maybe he was embarrassed about meeting me online. "So, what do you think, Zoe?"

"It looks like a grandfather's car." It was a 1994 Lincoln Continental, dark navy blue. The interior was all leather and polished chrome and plastic, and it was clean the way you'd expect a grandfather to keep a car clean. Vacuumed floors, spotless mats. It smelled stale.

Peter adjusted the mirrors and shifted into drive. He drove slowly, acting nonchalant about it, but he gripped the steering wheel tightly with both hands. "It runs pretty smooth."

"It feels fine back here," I said.

"Are you guys going anywhere?" Wolf asked.

"I might be driving Zoe back to Montreal. Think the car will make it?"

Lucy laughed, which made me worry. "I guess you'll see."

After we left the car with Wolf and Lucy, instead of heading into the city right away Peter took me on a walk toward the Hell Gate Bridge. The area was deserted and we could walk in the middle of the streets without worrying about oncoming traffic. We hopped over a stone ledge and passed a pile of discarded water bottles, some half-full of dark yellow urine.

It was interesting under the bridge—the graffiti, the river against the shore, the views of the city across the water. The bridge was imposing too, more severe-looking than the pretty latticework of the Brooklyn Bridge.

"I like visiting this kind of thing more than Times Square," I said.

"Me too." Peter paused. "Have you been to Niagara Falls?"

"When I was a kid. It's more like Times Square, though. It's pretty cheesy."

I'd been once with my parents and my father's relatives, his cousin George and George's wife, Katerina, when they'd visited from Greece. George was the closest I had to an uncle. I hadn't spoken to him in years.

"I've always wanted to go."

"Why?"

"I was conceived there."

"Ew. How do you know that?" I'd never thought to ask where I'd been conceived. I didn't really want to think about it.

"My dad told me. My parents were in an orchestra together at school before Mom dropped out. They played a concert in Buffalo, but snuck out on their own to visit the Falls instead of going to rehearsal."

"I've just been to the Canadian side."

"This was definitely in America."

"I don't think it's as cheesy."

"Do you mind if we stop on the drive over to Montreal?"

"It's not really on the way."

"Oh."

We had to look down while we walked under the bridge because there were so many rocks. Every so often, we would kick one to the other.

"It might be fun?" I said, convincing myself as the words came out.

"Really?"

"When do you want to go?"

"We don't have to leave right away; we should do more in the city."

We took the subway back into Manhattan, but I think we were both already planning a road trip. How could we not? Spending time with Peter sparked something inside me, tipped me in a new direction. He had so many things working his favour: his white-blond eyelashes, the shrunken head, the dumplings in Chinatown and now this, an escape plan, a new one.

ANNA

On our second-last day in France, we took the train to Versailles. Zoe called while we were en route, but I only felt the phone vibrate with a voice mail when we arrived.

"Hi, Mom," she said in the message. "Hope you're having a good time. We can talk when you get back. Don't worry about me; I'm doing fine." Her voice sounded small and far away, and I tried calling anyway, but her phone immediately went to voice mail. She was bad at keeping it charged, or she was screening my calls. At least she'd called me once, wherever she was.

By the time I put the phone away, the crowd of tourists with us on the train had fanned out. We weren't exactly sure how to get to the palace, like on our first day with the Eiffel Tower. I think we'd expected it to be more obvious, but we didn't see any signs. We eavesdropped on the couple beside us and started trailing them.

"*L'espionage*," Daniel said. "I know how to say that in French."

"It must be strange to live in a city with one singular defining attraction," I said as we walked. "Paris has the Eiffel Tower, but there are so many other things to pick as your favourite."

"I think you get used to it," Daniel said. "I knew someone who grew up in Niagara Falls, and he told me he only noticed them when visitors were in town."

The sun was shining, and before paying admission to

enter the palace, we walked around the gardens and out-side grounds. The Bassin d'Apollon was a statue of Apollo pulled out of the water by a half-dozen horses, as if he'd been sunk in the fountain and then figured out the way to escape toward dry land and sunlight. The fountains weren't running, so the water was still, Apollo looking more like a ghostly apparition than a statue. Daniel yawned.

"Don't tell me you're bored."

"I don't think that little cup of espresso was enough this morning."

"You want another one already?"

"Do you think there's a café here? In the Hall of Mirrors?"

Unsurprisingly there wasn't, so we turned around and explored the city of Versailles itself. We entered the first café we came across and took a table by the window. A heater on the floor blew warm air on my ankles.

"How are you feeling?" I asked. Daniel had been tossing and turning in the middle of the night.

"Fine." He nodded to my espresso. "Are you going to finish that?"

I pushed it toward him. There was a heaviness in the air. We were due for a conversation, not about our surround-ings or travelling or maps, but something more serious, like the fact that the ring was still in my purse. We'd also been unusually quiet with each other. The silence between us was even more profound when we were surrounded by people speaking French, their incomprehensible jabbering putting our soundlessness into sharp relief.

"What do you like best so far?" Daniel asked, apparently not interested in having a deeper conversation.

"Here? In Versailles?"

"Yeah."

"We haven't been here very long, I don't know. I think the statue of Apollo."

"It was impressive."

"It's not just that. Everything is impressive here."

"What did you like about it in particular?"

"I think I've dreamed it before."

"Oh?"

"When Niko died. I imagined something similar, not exactly horses pulling him out of the water, but mermaids."

"You're not really the mermaid type."

"Not mermaids, then, but sea creatures."

"So, is that what this is about?" Daniel shook his head.

"I don't know what you mean."

"The way you've been acting. Not talking. Is it because of Niko?"

"Of course not."

It didn't make sense to bring Niko up now—it was too late. I'd done too much and lived too long to be able to lay claim to any lingering guilt or regret or sadness. I didn't even think much about Niko anymore, consciously anyway. His memory wafted in sometimes, something ephemeral when I wasn't expecting that I'd learned to take in and then release. An exhale. If this was about Niko, and I had to explain it to Daniel, then I'd have to tell him everything. Not only did Daniel think that Niko and I had already begun divorce proceedings, but he also thought that Niko knew about him. He didn't; he had no idea he existed.

"Let's talk, then."

Daniel looked so earnest that my cheeks flushed, not just for me, but for him, too, for trying so hard. For always being so patient with me, not just on this trip, but for years. I worried that we were together only because we were in too

deep, that the effort our relationship had required at the beginning had tied us together unfairly. When it had started,
I was sure it was different from my relationship with Niko,
but now, sometimes, I felt as bogged down by the passage
of time and the resulting obligations as I had with Niko.

Even though I'd been gearing up for a discussion with
Daniel, I clammed up. What I really wanted was space. I
wanted a different kind of quiet, one that didn't make me
uncomfortable, one I could lose myself in without worrying about the person I was with. We'd visited Notre-Dame
Cathedral the day before, but the quiet was obscured by
the buzzing of other tourists. It would've been nice to walk
around the gardens in Versailles alone. Was it a bad sign
to wish these things with Daniel sitting right in front of
me? Bad timing, again. Or was I thinking this way because
the timing necessitated it, and Daniel was the one who'd
gotten the ball rolling?

I was, admittedly, suspicious of his proposal. Daniel's
wife had remarried a few months earlier, and when he'd
told me about it, it crossed my mind that we should, too,
but it must have made him mull it over more.

"Let's just go back," I said.

"To the hotel?"

"No, Versailles."

"Really?"

"Yes."

Neither of us budged. Finally I got up first. I was always
surprised by how easy it was to do something I didn't want
to do, to move forward. Daniel followed.

The clean lines of the palace of Versailles made me too
aware of my own tangles, and I quickly wanted to return to
Paris, where the scenery was messier, where it was easier to

accept that things could be knotted up and unmaintained and yet still beautiful.

We returned in the late afternoon, and when we were almost at the hotel, Daniel took the keys out of his pocket.

"Here," he said. "I'm going for a walk."

"Oh?" They dangled between us.

"You can come with me if you want."

He didn't really sound like he wanted me tagging along, though, so I took the keys. They weighed heavy, my pocket. "Will you be long?"

"No. Go, I'll join you later."

The owner was at the front desk when I came in. I asked for a recommendation for dinner, and he suggested a nearby restaurant. He wrote its name down on a slip of paper. His writing, cursive, was neat, as if from a school-boy's penmanship notebook.

In the room, I kicked off my shoes and pulled open the drapes for light. The man in the building across the street was at his desk, and I knocked on the window experimentally, but he didn't turn around.

After all this time of wanting to be alone, I was anxious about Daniel's walk. We weren't together all the time at home, and even here in Paris, I'd gone off on my own the first day. Now I was worried about Daniel using his time alone to *think*. I mean, to think the way I'd been thinking. It was scary knowing a person's internal life could influence your reality. While he was used to me ruminating over anything and everything, he didn't require as much self-reflection, so when he did something like this, I knew it was serious. I didn't want him scrutinizing our relationship or my behaviour, though.

My mother was afraid of being alone. I knew this from a very young age. If my father had to travel for work, she would make me share the bed with her, and when my father died first, I had the feeling she wouldn't live much longer without him, and I was right, she didn't. She came from a family of four sisters and wasn't used to being alone, but found herself in the smallest possible configuration of family. She used to tell me to have more than one child. She'd say it innocently, thinking it was good, solid advice, but it just made me uncomfortable.

One day, when Zoe was two years old, she was ambling through the house and tripped and smacked her forehead against the sharp edge of the coffee table. It was easy enough to keep knives and scissors and boiling kettles away from toddlers, but it turned out that the general architecture of everyday life—the height of a chair off the ground, unsuspecting, dangerous angles of a piece of furniture—was more difficult to protect your child from. There was a lot of blood, and for a minute I thought Zoe had pierced her eyeball, even though it was logistically impossible. Niko and I were both home, and we drove to the emergency room together, Zoe bleeding and crying, her face pressed against a towel on my blouse, Niko driving faster than I'd ever seen him. She got a few stitches and was back to being giggly and sweet by bedtime. When she woke up fussing more than usual at two in the morning, Niko got out of bed and soothed her until she fell asleep again.

"What a day," I said when he came back.

"I can't do it again."

"It happens all the time," I laughed. "Kids are tough. Zoe is tough."

"It's too much."

"You're tough, too."

"No, really. I don't think I can do it again."

I flipped onto my back and stuck a foot out from under the blankets because I was hot. "What do you mean?"

"Zoe is enough for me."

"She's enough for me, too," I replied defensively, but then I meant it. I hadn't really given much consideration to how many children we would have, but I'd assumed more than one, what my mother had advised. Now that it was planted, the idea of having one child, just Zoe, it wasn't so bad. We were both only children, anyway; we knew the upsides and downsides of it and could avoid repeating any mistakes our parents had made.

It was the pregnancy that started changing things between me and Niko. My dentist knew I was pregnant before him, for instance. I didn't do it on purpose, but I'd taken the test before a morning appointment. Niko had left early for work, and I hadn't mentioned it to him because part of me didn't think it was anything anyway.

The test came up immediately as positive. I called Niko at work, but he didn't answer, and since the news hadn't sunk in yet, I sped over to the appointment so that I wouldn't be late. As the dentist pulled out the lead vest for my X-rays, she said, "Oh, I have to ask if you're pregnant," and for a second I thought she'd deduced it, that I was broadcasting a signal that there was a baby growing inside of me.

"I am," I said, taken aback.

She hesitated. "Ah, we're not supposed to give pregnant women x-rays."

I didn't tell her that she was the first to know. She spent the rest of our appointment talking about her son while she scraped my teeth. I occasionally blinked in acknowledgement.

Niko didn't want to know if the baby was going to be a boy or a girl. "I might be disappointed," he said. "I'll be fine when I see the baby, but I don't have to know now."

He didn't tell me what he wanted more, although I suspected he'd prefer a boy. I, on the other hand, was dying to know. Or, at least, I wanted confirmation of what I knew. It was as if I had magnets in my brain—when I thought of the baby as a girl, the magnets came together, clicked. When I thought of the baby as a boy, they veered wildly apart. At the next appointment I went to by myself, I told the doctor my request, and he agreed to tell me without telling Niko. I was right: a girl. I burst into happy tears and thanked him.

That evening in bed we watched my stomach. The baby was big enough now that certain kicks and squirms poked my skin in a surreal show. "Look at her," I said a few times, until Niko asked why I was so sure it was a girl. I confessed.

"A girl," he said. "A girl." He touched my stomach and the baby calmed down. He pressed into it a few more times to jostle her back into action. "A girl."

These things—not knowing I was pregnant, not knowing the gender—prepared us for division in our relationship. Maybe it was just the inevitability of us getting to know each other more deeply. We'd been together for a year and a half when I got pregnant with Zoe, married six months, and there were quirks in our personalities that had started emerging. I preferred keeping certain things to myself, and he didn't prod too deeply for them, so we coexisted and grew apart inch by inch.

NIKO

Easter approached and the office was going to be closed for most of the week. George, Jimmy, Maria and Spiro had invited me to their respective Easter celebrations, but I didn't accept any of them right away. I'd been missing the freedom of having a car and thought about renting one over the holiday instead.

"Why don't we go on a trip together?" I asked Larissa. We were in bed, but she'd rolled over to the other single so we weren't touching. She'd been acting coolly toward me since the encounter with George.

"You're funny."

"Can you get one night off?"

"No."

"The store won't even be open over Easter."

"I'll have work to do anyway."

"Why don't you call in sick? You must get sick sometimes. You need a break."

"I don't know."

I asked again before she left that night, and she still didn't answer yes or no. I wrote it off until a few days later, when she told me that her sister might be able to cover a day.

"Does your sister know about me?"

"Yes." She said it as if it wasn't a big deal. "Well, she doesn't know your full name or where you live. Where should I tell her we're going?"

"Where do you want to go? You choose."

"Meteora," she said after a moment.

"Really? Isn't it...religious?"

"So what?"

Meteora was known for small monasteries perched high on top of a series of sandstone cliffs. Larissa had never expressed a religious side, and Albania was an atheist country, so I was surprised she was interested. They were beautiful structures regardless of beliefs, I suppose. The monasteries had been built hundreds of years ago, and back then the only way monks could access them was by being hauled up by a precarious system of nets and pulleys. If a net broke, a monk died, and the act would be chalked up to God's will. Today paths had been built so that anyone could drive right up to their front doors, and only a handful of monks still lived in them.

It was as good a choice as any. Larissa's sister agreed to cover for her, and I told George, Jimmy, Maria and Spiro that I had plans. Jimmy tried to convince me otherwise, but the others probably guessed who I'd be with and didn't comment.

Larissa and I left Athens early on Friday morning. She'd made tiropita for breakfast, and it was still warm and greasy, the pastry flaking in my lap as I drove, the cheese still melting. The roads getting out of the city were clogged with people on similar trips, but then there was a break in traffic and we were free. We drove steadily until the cliffs appeared, tall rock formations that looked alien compared with the rest of their surroundings, like they'd been shaped out of the Play-Doh Zoe used to play with.

Easter weekend was busy. There were lines of tour buses along the curved thin roads, and tourists poured out of them carrying cameras and guidebooks. We chose a monastery with the smallest crowd, one that required a half-kilometre hike uphill to enter. The path was bursting with signs of spring: dark green foliage snaking up between the rocks, flowering bushes along the side, flying insects buzzing above us. The cliffs around us were the colour of wet wood.

A teenager in jeans charged us two euros each to enter. The walls of the monastery were bare stone or covered in peeling white paint, and a monk had also painted a mural of Jesus, now badly chipped with age. A net, a grid of leather straps and ropes, was piled on the floor next to a hole in one of the walls, the former entrance/exit. I peeked down and doubted the monks had truly been at peace with the risks of being pulled up such a great height in that flimsy, archaic contraption, but maybe religion helped them accept unacceptable things.

In the chapel, a table by the altar was littered with scraps of paper. I picked one up and someone had written in a slanted, pained handwriting, *Petros, my father*. They were names of people for the monks to pray for. I wondered if Zoe would ever do that for me. Pray. I hoped not.

My parents hadn't been religious, but every so often my mother could take it to an extreme, although she was more superstitious than religious. If we'd been alive hundreds of years earlier, I'm sure we would've been members of a cult living at the foot of a mountain. It wasn't hard to imagine my parents making sacrifices and spilling blood in supplication to the gods.

My mother arranged an exorcism for me when I was six years old. So much of my life is cloudy until then, but the day of the exorcism stands out clearly. I'd been chronically sick, wracked with a persistent cold and cough I could never shake, the type of middling illness that gets you labelled as sickly compared to your peer group. This haze was pierced with memories of camphor and metallic-tasting tinctures I would have to drink before going to bed and taste at the back of my throat until the following morning. I don't remember my childhood dreams, but I remember those tastes.

Once in Canada, a co-worker of mine had been worried about his son's allergies. He'd sent him to an allergist who performed scratch tests on his back to isolate every single thing that was harming him. The test sounded so precise and efficient, something my parents would've never conceived of doing even if a doctor had suggested it. Case in point: when my doctor couldn't find anything overtly wrong with me, my mother pursued the matter with a priest.

I got scared when he opened my bedroom door and came swishing in with his long black robe and grey beard. The smell of church clung to him—incense, mothballs—a smell I associated more with death than God. He sprinkled me with Holy Water and chanted from a Bible while my parents hovered to the side. I felt paralyzed, afraid to move or cough, and then I started to sweat, feverishly, enough that my mother later changed the sheets. After my parents died, I found the rosary the priest had given me when it was over at the back of a desk drawer.

I've always suspected that I was cursed. Are some people predisposed to bad luck? If it's one day proven to be genetic, then I inherited it from my father. When I was a child, I noticed that bad things, often happened to him. Not necessarily big things but, for example, he frequently lost items that were important to him—papers, lighters, his watch.

As I grew older, I had similar phases of misfortune. When a consecutive string of unfortunate events felt like more than just a coincidence, I'd blame him. I couldn't do anything to turn my luck around; I would have to let it drift over me like a fog until it cleared, and while the majority of the curse was expelled that sweaty day of the exorcism, some trace amounts remained. I didn't tell anyone that I believed in this—exorcisms, luck, curses—but sometimes I agreed with my parents that that an external force shaped my life.

When I met Anna, I was at the tail end of one of my bad-luck periods. My first job had ended abruptly, and I was worried I would have to slink back to Greece. If the Onassis and Kennedy marriage had been a good sign for my arrival in North America, events that came after their wedding signalled bad news: Onassis's son died first while I was abroad, and then he did, too, at only sixty-nine.

When I moved to Toronto, I wasn't dating anyone, and was embarrassed by my living arrangements: a single room in a house with a shared kitchen and bathroom. It was fine when I'd been a student, but I was now well into my thirties. I'd chosen to live in the Greek part of town because it was comforting seeing street signs in the language I grew up with, but I was ready to cut the cord. I moved, found a new job, met Anna. How could these drastic changes not have been at least partially nudged into place by a change in luck? I thought of Anna as a good-luck charm—there was something delicate and precious about her. She had long hair that she would wind into a bun at the top of her head, leaving her neck bare and smooth. She wore loose blouses and long skirts and big earrings, and her wrists in my hands were the perfect size.

I found Larissa in the courtyard behind the monastery. I stood behind her, and she smiled and touched my arm lightly. The air smelled like it had a texture, like wheat spores had been released into the air or like sap from the trees had thickened it. I rarely saw trees in Athens; I didn't realize it until I was surrounded by them. When we left, we walked back slowly to the car, holding hands.

That night while we were eating dinner, I told her that I wanted to marry her.

"You're already married," she said, although not unkindly, not mockingly, not sadly, just stating the fact.

"If I wasn't married." I felt the same as how I'd felt when I'd proposed to Anna, like I had an abundance of good fortune and happiness and that it should be stretched out to larger proportions. I knew I wanted to marry her as soon as we'd met. She didn't mind that I was older. I proposed quickly because I was afraid that if I waited too long, she would change her mind, and then, luckily, she accepted.

"But you are. That's all that counts."

I wondered if I could marry Larissa in Greece and stay married to Anna in Canada. I still loved Anna, but I'd moved abroad knowing she wasn't happy about it, and started a relationship with another woman. Was my definition of love skewed? The truth was that I was surprised every time Anna ended a phone call without bringing up the topic of divorce again. Maybe it was a test, an unspoken separation to figure things out for ourselves.

The next morning Larissa was anxious to get back early, and so we headed toward the hovering smog above Athens, away from the cliffs. We'd been away just under twenty-four hours, but it was the longest uninterrupted stretch of time we'd ever spent together.

I dropped her off at her apartment first and then, magically, found a parking spot less than a half-block from my place. Whatever I'd done had been the right ritual for the gods: I had invoked a perfect parking spot, the perfect ending to a perfect weekend.

ZOE

Peter and I walked over to the Met. The streets were starkly different from the Bronx, but a few blocks later the novelty of the difference dissipated. After wandering around New York, I felt like, in its hugeness, the city was endless repetition, the same stores selling the same things, new faces replacing the ones I'd just seen. It was easier to process in small chunks—some time spent within the radius of a few blocks made it appear small and manageable again. I wanted a unique impression of the city, but there was so much to wade through to make it my own.

At the Met we started in the section with replicas of rooms from different periods. The lights were dimmed low to protect the antique furniture and textiles. If a flash of sunlight appeared, I imagined that everything would crumble to dust, leaving only the wooden bones of the furniture and a pile of nails.

In one of the sculpture halls, we sat on a marble bench among the dozens of statues of Greek gods missing various appendages. That first time I went to Greece with my parents, we'd gone to the Acropolis and the archaeological museum to see these kinds of sculptures, but I was too young to appreciate them. The second time, for my father's funeral, I remember being in the car at night and seeing the Acropolis lit up on the hill, the dark blue sky against it. It had looked more like a diorama than something I'd visited before. If I'd squinted hard enough or looked at it with bin-oculars would I have seen people up there, or gods? Maybe.

I liked sitting close to Peter. He awkwardly stroked my hair, which was limp and flat from travelling, and I leaned over and so did he, and we kissed. He tasted like cinnamon gum. We kissed until a guard came over and cleared his throat. For the rest of our time at the museum, we held hands, getting used to the feel of each other's skin. I saw a Georgia O'Keeffe painting I'd never seen. It had some of the dusty rose I was used to in her work, but this one was black and grey. This is what I wanted when I'd left Montreal: to see something familiar, but different. New.

We sat out on the steps afterwards, and I ate a knish while Peter made a few calls.

"I'll have insurance for the car by tomorrow," he said when he was done. "Are we going to go?"

I looked at the street vendors, the tourists. A swarm of pigeons ignored us and pecked at crumbs discarded from the surrounding vendors. These things, the individual com-ponents that made up New York City, would be here the next time I came—I didn't have to unlock any mysteries of the city now; I could leave and, later, return. "Okay."

"Really?"

"Really."

Peter stuck out his hand and we shook on it.

The next morning I packed up my things. I was wearing the same jeans I'd been wearing since arriving, although after the Met I'd ducked into a few stores and bought a grey long-sleeved shirt and some earrings, silver and dangly. In my backpack I still had clean tights, socks, a few T-shirts, a sweater, a jean skirt. I had some cash, most of it Canadian.

I didn't like how American money was all the same colour, no difference between a dollar bill and a hundred. I had the *Sleeping Gypsy* postcard and I still had Bill from Albany's phone number. And I had *The Solitary Woman*.

We had to take the train back to the Bronx, but didn't spend much time with Wolf and Lucy, just picked up the car keys and threw our bags in the trunk. Peter had brought the shrunken head and put it on the dashboard for good luck.

Niagara Falls wasn't too far away. A seven-hour drive, easy, if we went straight. We would spend the night and then head over to Montreal. I wasn't sure if Peter could stay with Susie and in our room, but we'd figure it out on the way over. I was starting to trust that things fell into place if you gave them enough time.

We'd both preferred the idea of using an actual, physical map to relying on directions printed out from the Internet, so we'd purchased one and traced our route out with a red marker the night before. I held it in my lap as we crossed the George Washington Bridge and tried to memorize the highway numbers. I-95, I-81, I-90.

For the first hour we talked only about traffic, merging lanes. Peter was serious at the wheel, his brow furrowed in concentration. He had the faintest freckles. We hadn't kissed since the Met, and I wanted to touch his cheek or hold his hand. I felt shy, though, and it would be distracting. He looked nervous, too—both hands gripped the wheel tightly.

It didn't take long for the concrete of New York City to feel like a bizarre dream. I looked out the window at the miles of open fields around us, the treelines and solitary houses, and this was when I really started to feel far away from my life, from everything that had happened over the past few months, years, forever.

"I can drive when you need a break," I told Peter. "I haven't driven in a while, but I can do it."

When I got my driver's licence, one of the first places I drove was to a psychic at a nearby strip mall. I'd noticed the sign when I went to the grocery store with my mom and had always wanted to try it out. It cost twenty dollars for a ten-minute reading. I brought Emily with me and she went first, and when she was done she had the biggest grin on her face. I'd waited in a small room that smelled like nag champa, watching fish dart around an aquarium in quick, jerky circles.

When it was my turn, the psychic took my hand, looked into my eyes, scrunched up her forehead and asked if I'd recently experienced loss. I burst into tears and immediately hated myself for giving it away so quickly. It was almost the fifth anniversary of my father's death, and the date made me queasy. I'd been treating the visit as an experiment, curious to see if some people really could read minds or predict the future. I wondered how much this so-called psychic could figure out on her own, if she could really tell if I was sad or not, and then I'd gone ahead and made it easy for her. She took my other hand and told me that everything was going to be okay, but that she could tell that my aura was "damaged." She made it sound like it was a vessel of some sort—a boat?—with a leak in it. I was walking around with a giant deflated aura, and I'd have to work hard to make it healthy again, to plump it up. She recommended a type of tea, and also assured me that my love life looked promising, but only added that because my tears continued to stream down my cheeks. I couldn't stop them right away. I washed my face in her bathroom, and for the rest of the day I smelled her lavender-scented soap on my skin and incense in my hair.

"My dad taught me how to drive when I spent a summer with a few years ago," Peter told me. He saw his father once or twice a year. They rarely spoke on the phone, although they would exchange e-mails, his dad sending long missives while he killed time in an airport or during a rehearsal. I asked him if he missed him, when he was a kid.

"Yeah," he said. "Sometimes. Do you see your dad often?"

I knew I'd told him about my father in the past, but hadn't mentioned anything about him recently, which was funny, given how much I'd been thinking about him on this trip. I hadn't even shown him my grandmother's book.

"No," I said. "Well, he's dead."

When Peter blushed, his entire face turned a deep pink, including his ears, the tips and lobes. "I knew that. I forgot; I'm sorry."

"It's okay."

"Do you miss him?"

I wasn't asked this question often because wasn't it implied that I did? I worried that I thought about him too much. It wasn't constant, but there were periods when it was stronger than others. When I concentrated on what exactly I missed about him, it was hard to pin down. His presence, I guess, the solidity of him. I remembered that more clearly than the way he looked.

Often when I thought about my father, what came to me were questions. Why did he really go back to Athens? Why didn't he insist that we go back with him? Did he feel guilty for leaving me and my mother, or at least just me? I sometimes thought I knew the answer to these questions, but it was frustrating that I didn't, and couldn't, know for sure.

"I do miss him," was all I said to Peter. "We have to take the next exit."

We stopped at a gas station in the Catskills. When I came out of the bathroom, Peter was on his phone. I hung back and tried to look busy. He was talking to his mother about Wolf's car and how he had money saved up and yes, he had insurance, and he could afford it, and now we were going to Montreal, just for a few days. From his tone of voice and his answers, I could tell that she was confused.

"I bought you a piece of pie," he said when he was done. "They were selling slices by the cash when I paid for the gas." He held out a Styrofoam plate covered in plastic wrap. The slice was a little crushed, but pale yellow fruit oozed out the side. "It's apple."

"Thank you." I hugged him and he wrapped his arms around me and we stood like that for a minute, the piece of pie getting more and more flattened between my hands.

"I didn't tell my mom I was doing this," he said when we were back in the car.

"I didn't tell mine I was going to New York until I arrived either," I said. "She wasn't pleased."

"I don't know what the big deal is. We're adults."

Peter saying this made me feel like we weren't really. That the car was a prop for our game, like we'd visited our grandparents for the day and snuck into the garage to pretend to drive while the real adults were inside having a drink.

We pulled into a motel off a highway exit when it got dark and we wanted to rest. It was called the Pine Tree Inn and there were trees out front, but they weren't pines.

"Seventy-five dollars," a man with a moustache told us after we rang a bell until he emerged from wherever he was hiding.

"What about fifty?" I asked, remembering negotiating

with Bill in Albany. "In cash."

"Sounds good to me." He wrote out a receipt with a green pen, his fingers nicotine-stained and gave us a key to a room that smelled like stale cigarettes.

I wore a slip to bed, which was kind of like a dress, not really lingerie, just something pretty I'd also purchased the day before. It reminded me of sea foam, airy and light. When I'd put it on, Peter's eyes had bugged out for a second. He touched my bare thighs first and kissed my shoulders. Having sex in the motel was exciting, the act of it. It wasn't just plain sex and it wasn't anything cheesy like making love, either; it was fucking in its purest sense, learning these perfect, primal things about each other's bodies and mouths in straightforward ways.

Peter fell asleep right away. I couldn't, so I got up to get my notebook. The room was cold. I tried turning up the heat on the radiator, but nothing happened. I cranked it to the highest setting until it started banging around.

The neon of the motel sign leaked through the sheer curtains, bathing the room in flickering green. It was just light enough for me to write without turning on a lamp. I listed everything I'd done since leaving Montreal and it added up to three pages. I was going to sketch a picture of the slip I'd bought, but after writing it down, liked the look of the page without the picture included, like this:

I bought this

in sea foam.

"What are you doing?" Peter mumbled from bed. "Come back."

I put my notebook away and climbed back into bed and pressed my forehead into Peter's back, right between his shoulder blades. He sighed in his sleep, and I breathed in his smell.

ANNA

Niko and I went to Greece for our honeymoon, and at the time I thought it was the beginning of frequent trips over the course of our shared life, but the next time I went was when we brought Zoe to meet her grandparents when she was four, and then I didn't go again until Niko's funeral. We'd stopped accompanying him because as his parents got older, he went more out of duty than vacation, usually off-season, when I was busy at work or while Zoe was still in school. His parents were becoming senile and he insisted that there was nothing interesting for us to do stuck in Athens. Why waste money on plane tickets?

Our honeymoon had been perfect, though. We went in August, when Athens was empty and at its hottest. We walked off the plane in the middle of the tarmac, and my legs wobbled on the stairs when the shimmering heat of the city slapped against us. There were dogs in the airport sleeping just beyond the luggage carousels and pigeons pecking at crumbs on the ground. Years later, when the airport moved to a newer, cleaner location, Niko told me he missed being greeted by those feral animals.

His parents didn't speak much English. When we arrived at their apartment, his mother grasped my hands and told me how much she loved me. She insisted that I call her by her first name, Zaharoula, which somehow translated to Jackie in English. I couldn't bring myself to call her Jackie, and Zaharoula didn't roll off my North American tongue, so I didn't call her anything. Her eyes were bright with tears and she called me "doll." *Koukla*. I always remembered this word because Niko would call Zoe this, his little *koukla*.

Zaharoula was a poet. She'd sat me down and shown me a book she'd written, along with clippings of other published poems. Some of them were pressed between pages of bigger books, the way one saves leaves in autumn, and she pulled them out carefully so that I could examine them up close. There was even an English translation of her book, which I tried to read while Niko and his parents talked loudly above my head.

"I hate that book," Niko said. "A vanity press released it and made her pay for the privilege."

"Can we take it back with us?"

"It's the only copy left, but I'll ask."

I didn't insist on packing it in my suitcase—I'd taken for granted that I'd be back another time to get it then. As it was, I never got a copy, and I don't know what happened to the book when Niko sold their apartment.

I'd hoped I could learn things about Niko from his mother's poems. "She didn't write about me," he told me once, but I wasn't convinced. If I wrote poems, they would surely include Zoe in some way. I couldn't believe that Zaharoula didn't write about her only son, but maybe a true artist knows how to keep the personal out of her work, or at least how to disguise it. I wasn't sure. Before Niko left for Greece, I thought about the book again, and then forgot about it until Zoe found a copy of the Greek version, the one Niko had brought with him when he first moved away.

"I'll try to translate it," she'd said, and she'd sounded so determined that I didn't doubt she could do it. I didn't know how far she'd gotten with it, but I'd ask her about it the next time I saw her.

Niko's parents wanted us to stay with them for our honeymoon, but Niko had thankfully booked a hotel downtown.

One morning, when he had to look after some paperwork at the bank, he told me his mother wanted to take me somewhere. "You don't have to go," he said, but I agreed to, even if we couldn't understand each other.

Zaharoula was comfortable chatting with me no matter how mute I remained. In response I would smile and nod my head and say something in English, a non sequitur, and after some time it felt like we were having a running conversation. When you don't know a language, you can't even tell where one word ends and the next begins, each phrase a loop of unfamiliar syllables and tones.

I'd worn my bathing suit under my dress, as she'd instructed, and we took a bus to Lake Vouliagmeni, a brackish body of water not far from the sea, a forty-five-minute ride outside the downtown core. We passed beaches, but she insisted on this lake, and even if I wanted to go elsewhere, I wasn't sure how to tell her.

"Look how beautiful it is," Zaharoula said, or at least that's what I assumed she said by the sweep of her arm and the tone of pride in her voice when we entered. The water was more green than blue, and the lake was surrounded by tall, sheer cliffs. There was no beach, just a cement patio. People walked around in robes or in their bathing suits, while others floated in the lake. There was no splashing, no running, no loud voices; everything was calm. Zaharoula took my hand when we waded in. Dozens of tiny fish swarmed our feet and nibbled at our toes. They were eating the dead skin.

The water was warm. Niko had explained to me that some people thought the lake had healing powers. It was supposedly radioactive, charged by the surrounding rocks and the sun. It was fed by the sea via a network of caverns beneath the cliffs, but no one could trace their precise route. Those who had tried had gotten lost underwater, run out of oxygen from their tanks and died. I floated in it and wondered what it could be fixing in me. I felt peaceful. Tingly.

We'd spent the rest of our honeymoon in Spetses. On the ferry ride over, we'd sat outside on uncomfortable benches, and salt water had coated my teeth.

"Why is that?" I asked him.

"It's because your mouth is open," he said, and it was true, I couldn't stop smiling.

We rented a motorbike on the island and kept it parked in the courtyard of our hotel. The closest beaches weren't very good, so we'd take the bike. The best beach was at the bottom of a cove a few kilometres east of the port. It was too steep to ride down, so people left their bikes at the top, unchained, and then hiked.

I remember lying on the sand by the water, closing my eyes and feeling like I was being held, enveloped. Later, when I rinsed the salt water off my body, tiny whirlpools of sand gathered around the bathtub drain, refusing to be washed away completely. It would stick to my feet and get caught in our sheets and rub against our bare skin when we made love, and I would taste it in my mouth, the grittiness of the dirt combined with the salt from the sea and our skin, but it never felt unclean, just elemental.

I often wondered if Niko thought about me during his last days. His accident happened in Spetses, and I never knew why he'd chosen to go there.

Niko's cousin George was the one to call me from Athens to tell me about it. I'm still grateful it was him and not a stranger, some nameless official speaking broken English. I'd met George more often than any of Niko's relatives. He and Katerina had also visited us in Canada when Zoe was very young. Zoe had liked him and the way he would tease her and carry her on his shoulders. I knew Niko had been seeing George a lot in Athens, but I hadn't spoken to him myself in a long time.

The first thing he'd said was, "I have bad news about Niko."

"Who?" I'd asked. I'd meant *what*.

"Your husband, Anna." Actually, he'd said *My Anna* by adding the Greek word *mou* to the end of my name, stretching it into three syllables. He said it to be gentle. I got stuck on the word *husband*, though. Niko and I may have been separated geographically and emotionally, too, but when George called, Niko was indeed still my husband. He had no clue about Daniel, couldn't name him or picture him. He had no proof. At that moment, I wanted Niko, him, whole. *Fine, stay in Greece*, I thought, *but you're still my husband*. There was something binding about continuing to think of him as that—a husband—an invocation that could potentially conjure him back. I'd felt it so viscerally that an irrational part of me still wouldn't let it go completely.

After the phone call, what scared me most was having to watch Zoe's face crumple into tears at the news. The thought of watching that storm of emotions made me numb. I stayed awake, called George every hour to find out what else he knew. What if it was a false alarm? What if he'd been rescued in the meantime? When I couldn't deny it anymore and had no choice but to tell Zoe, I braced myself for the sobs.

She was in bed, still hugged by sleep. Her face wrinkled into a question mark and her eyes got cloudy, but she didn't cry. And this made me feel worse. I'd been steeling myself for tears, not silence. More than grief and shock, I felt like a failure. A complete and total failure of a mother, a wife, a human. I wasn't even good at being a mistress.

When Zoe did cry, when I found her, it was gasping and silent and awful, like she was drowning. I tried to wipe her tears away, but her face was sticky, tacky. I missed her sweet, childhood tears. Clear and salty, like sea water sluicing off skin when you emerge from a swim.

Niko's accident had happened on a boat he'd rented from a fisherman on the island who'd said that Niko had looked happy and relaxed. The tiny dinghy looked flimsy when I saw a picture of it. How anything like that could be safe in the sea was hard to swallow, but this man had been using it for years without incident. The harbour was filled with boats just like it, and apparently no one ever died in them. It was just bad luck.

NIKO

Not long after Easter, my washing machine stopped working. I opened the door, and greyish water sloshed out the front, the clothes inside soaked and heavy. I pulled the machine away from the wall and reconnected the hose, but the water wouldn't drain. I hauled the wet clothes out to the balcony, and as I was wringing out a shirt, Maria peeked her head around the corner.

"What are you doing?"

"My washing machine broke."

"Elly has a friend who fixes machines—he fixed ours a few months ago. He's cheap."

I bought bread from Elly less frequently after she'd been outside one evening when Larissa and I were about to enter my building. Something about the way she'd looked at me when I'd greeted her made me uncomfortable, and then when I went to buy bread the next day, she'd acted more aloof than usual. Still, on Maria's suggestion I stopped by to see her after work. Before I had the chance to say anything, she was talking business.

"I called my friend," she said. "He can come over tonight to fix your washing machine."

"What?"

"Maria told me."

"So he's coming...tonight? In a few hours?"

"You'll be home, won't you?"

"Can he call me first?"

"He'll just come over. I'll buzz and let you know when he's here."

There was no convincing her to book a proper appointment, so I went to my apartment and waited. When my door buzzed late, after nine, I assumed it was Larissa, but it was actually him.

He was Albanian and spoke little Greek. My clothes had dried stiffly on the line from the residual detergent, and I held out a shirt as proof. He nodded and got to work, and when he was almost finished, the door buzzed again. This time it was Larissa. She jumped when she noticed him. Rather than explain what he had done in Greek, he spoke to her in Albanian and she translated for me. He'd managed to fix a broken pump, but it would have to be replaced eventually. In the meantime it would work for a bit longer. I paid him and he left.

As soon as the door closed behind him, Larissa was angry. "You should have warned me that there'd be someone here. You could've called."

"I didn't know he was coming so late. And you told me not to call you anymore."

"You can call me when it's important."

"You didn't mind so much when George came by."

"That was different."

"How so?"

"He was your problem, not mine. Too many people have been seeing us lately; it's not right. I shouldn't even be here now."

"Why? No one cares." I said this, but doubted myself—people were starting to care, and their opinions were smothering me as well. Our world, which had been expanded by our trip to Meteora, was now contracting, constrained by the knowledge that our relationship was no longer a sweet secret we had to keep.

"You don't understand."

Larissa left anyway, and I put my clothes back into the machine. It worked, but noisily. I listened to the clothes tumble around from my bed.

A few days later, after a long meeting that had left me with a headache, the phone rang soon after I came home. It was Zoe.

"Shouldn't you be in school?" I asked. It was about noon in Canada.

"I'm sick today."

"Where's your mother?"

"She's not home. I'm fine on my own."

I knew Anna would have stayed home if Zoe had really needed her, and she sounded well enough on the phone, but it still made me sad to think of her alone in the house, probably still in her pyjamas, her hair matted and tangled. It was hard for me to think of her as anything but a little girl, even if she was a teenager now. The image pinned in my mind was at a different stage.

"Can you get your mother to call me when she gets home tonight?" I asked. Zoe agreed and then started telling me about a geography presentation she was missing. I listened to her voice more than her words.

I sometimes wondered how to talk to my daughter, the right way to do it. Usually I just let her speak, and she would fill in the gaps. I still remember my relief when she said her first words and then started stringing sentences together. I was amazed when she could look at us and say exactly what she was thinking. Up until then, I'd been hopeless at guessing what she wanted. Anna had been better at interpreting her cries, the tones of them. She tried explaining them to me ("Hear that? It's higher-pitched. It means something she wants was taken away from her."), but I couldn't distinguish the differences. They were just baby cries and hard to listen to for any length of time, even from my own daughter.

I tried to remember how my parents used to speak to me. Because they were writers, people thought we had philosophical conversations at home, but they kept their philosophizing to their writing. I was more familiar with the economics of their writing than the content of it. As I got older, the distinct lack of income coming from their artistic pursuits concerned me most. Because my mother was a housewife, there was nothing unusual about her staying at home, even though, more often than not, my grandmother supplied us with meals when she was caught up in a project. However, my father, who was supposed to be the breadwinner, wasn't bringing much in either, and I sensed it without requiring any access to bank statements. As I got older and thought seriously about moving away, I knew I would need money to go, and if they weren't going to be able to help me, I would have to do something about it myself.

After my mother published *The Solitary Woman*, she received a small but consistent stream of letters from people who appreciated her work. They came mainly from ordinary people from Greece, but sometimes something would arrive on more official letterhead. There was a congratulatory letter from the British School of Classical Studies in London, and, even more exotic, a typed note from a university in South America. *Facultad de Filosofía, Centro de Estudios Bizantinos Neohelénicos, Santiago, Chile.*

I was happy when I read these letters, not just because they meant someone respected her work, but also because it could potentially lead to more money.

And then she received a letter from a press in the United States proposing to publish an English translation. The letter was written half in Greek and half in English, and my parents asked me to read the English part over for them. They knew a few words here and there, and owned a handful of English books—Hemingway especially, because I suspected his simple style was easier to understand. I, on the other hand, had taken English courses for years. My certificate from the Greek-American Cultural Institute was framed and hanging in the front hall. My parents were tickled with the stamped inscription, *Progress: Excellent.*

The letter from the press was odd. Instead of an advance, my mother would have to send them a cheque for publication. The Greek edition hadn't required the contribution of a single drachma on her part. My parents were so swept away with the thought of her being published in English in America that they mailed off the cheque without hesitation, even though I told them that something about the transaction didn't feel right.

The publisher was based in an office in Auburn, New York. To them, "New York" was the operative part of the address. The state was considered interchangeable with the city, and they pictured skyscrapers, rush hour, taxi cabs and lunch appointments. When I moved and became familiar with the geography of America, I learned that Auburn was nothing like New York City—it had none of the glamour, none of the clout. It was just a small town.

When the books arrived, I was intrigued. They were cheaply printed and not as nice as the original Greek version. My mother's photo appeared on the inside flap of the jacket, but it had been a small passport photo blown up to blurry proportions. There was a garish drawing of a Doric column on the cover and in large Greek-style script, the kind often used for Greek fast-food restaurants, the title had been switched from *The Solitary Woman* to something more official, *The Anthologized Poetry of Jackie Kiriakos*. My mother's name, Zaharoula, was uncommon in America and its anglicized version, *Jackie*, was in vogue, but who had told her to change it? My mother? The press? I was also fascinated by her biography, printed under the photo. It was much longer than the one in the Greek edition:

> *Jackie Kiriakos was born in Athens, Greece, and is a graduate of the University of Athens, where she studied philology and recitation. She contributes to Greek literary periodicals and newspapers of prominence. She is deeply inspired by Greek tradition and by the value and deep sense of internal life and traces the sanctity of inner courage against the latticework of the external world. Plain sincerity, pure humanity, lyrical passion, keen insight, extreme tenderness and most refined feelings characterize this true Neo-Hellenic voice.*

"It's nice, isn't it?" she asked.

"Did you write that?" I thought the praise was excessive. "Is that what a biography is supposed to look like?"

"Yes," she told me. "People in America want to know that what they're buying is worth it before they spend their money."

Because of my relative expertise in English, my mother wanted my help to review the translation. "Shouldn't we have done this before it was published?" I asked, but she assured me it was normal. We went through each poem one by one. First she listened to me read a poem out loud in English—my accent was better, too—and then I would connect it word by word to the corresponding Greek. The easiest poems were the short ones, only a line or two. We did those first. The longer poems were harder, and my mother would write down the words she didn't know and then obsess over their definitions in the dictionary to confirm that she was happy with them.

It reminded me of the comprehension exercises I would do in my English courses, where I would have to read a story or poem and then answer a series of tedious questions at the end. If it was a poem about waves crashing on the shore, the textbook would ask, "What lines in the poem make you hear the sound of the waves beating against the rocks?" I would pencil in the appropriate answers as quickly as possible. It was harder to rush through the exercise with my mother hanging off my arm, studying every letter, every line break.

The translator was a woman named Maria T. Peters and she lived in Maryland. Her biography was also included in the book, but more prominently on the back cover. You had to open the book to read about my mother, but simply flip it over to read about the translator. Even Maria T. Peters's photo was better, smooth-skinned, hair pinned up elegantly, face turned three-quarters toward the camera, demure.

Maria T. Peters was born in Athens, Greece, later came to the United States, and is now a naturalized American citizen. She studied English at the University of Maryland, hence her excellent command of the language, which is here applied to the transcription of the poetry of Mrs. Kiriakos. An English teacher and freelance writer, Maria T. Peters has contributed her studies and critical essays in English and Greek to various newspapers and magazines in America. It must be emphasized that Mrs. Peters has not simply translated Mrs. Kiriakos' work; she has transcribed the original text in a magnificent, personal way. Between the foreign reader and the author stands the adaptor, the translator. Without her thorough understanding of both languages, the quality of the original effort would have been lost. Maria T. Peters is married and lives in Annapolis, Maryland, with her husband, Fred E. Peters, an engineer.

My mother's bio had seemed like too much, but the translator's was even more excessive. My parents' library was primarily based on the work of translators. They loved Victor Hugo especially, and Flaubert. After reading Maria T. Peters's biography, I scanned translations I could find in the apartment to see if the translators got as much billing as the author. They didn't. In some cases, their name wasn't even listed, and there was definitely no mention of the importance of their work. I was embarrassed for my parents for being so proud of what seemed, to me, a scam.

My mother suggested that I contact Maria T. Peters when I moved. I refused, and I also refused to take a copy of the translation. When I left for America, the money I carried with me came from Alexander, not my parents. The cheque they sent to the press wasn't for a staggering amount, but it was still money they could have contributed to my future. I would have never put Zoe in that position.

The phone rang again a few hours later. It was Anna.

"How's Zoe?" I asked.

"She's fine. She had a bit of a temperature, but it's lower now. She just needed to rest."

"And how are you?"

"I'm not sick."

"I mean, otherwise."

"I'm fine, too, I guess."

"Really?"

"I don't know." She paused. "How are you?"

"I'm not sure either."

"Oh?"

"Things are hard these days."

"You've finally gotten yourself into some trouble?"

"What do you mean?" I wondered if she'd heard something about Larissa or Calypso, but how was that even possible? George would have never said anything.

"I just assumed that eventually something would happen to make you admit that this whole situation is hard."

"It doesn't have to be hard, though. I never wanted it to be."

"Are you happy there?"

I looked around my apartment. It was so dusty. I'd swept a few times since moving, but hadn't really dusted any other surface, and dirt from the balcony was migrating its way in. Larissa often curled her nose at the mess and refused to walk barefoot around the apartment. At certain angles you could see the smudges of my feet on the dark marbled floors. A few dirty plates were on the desk since I hadn't washed in a while and, unlike in Toronto, I didn't have a dishwasher. I should've hired someone to help clean. It would probably have been an Albanian. "I'm fine here. You're still going to visit, right?" I asked.

Anna's voice wobbled. "Niko, I don't know."

"What do you mean? You have to."

"Maybe Zoe should just go on her own."

"Don't you miss me, though? Just a little bit?"

"I don't have the energy to talk about this."

"We haven't talked about anything since I left."

She sighed. Her voice steadied itself. "I don't know what to do."

"About what?"

"About us, Niko. About this, all of this."

I could picture her swinging her arms around, gesturing in large circles, implying not just us, but our world, our life. I thought of her hands, their softness. When she was pregnant, her fingers swelled up and she'd had to take off her wedding ring during her third trimester. The swelling went down, but the ring never fit comfortably again, so she'd stopped wearing it on her hand and put it on a chain around her neck instead. She didn't like wearing rings anyway. I didn't either, so I never wore mine, but now it felt more significant that both of us were traipsing around, ringless.

"Do we have to do anything?" I asked.

"I think we do, but I'm too tired to figure that out right now."

"Let's talk tomorrow then."

"I can't tomorrow."

"Why not?"

"I just can't."

"Fine. When will we talk?"

"Soon."

This conversation was closest to the discussion I'd been expecting since I'd come to Greece: a direct acknowledgement that something was wrong. I knew Anna was approaching a breaking point, and instead of reassuring her or speeding it up, I'd agreed to just wait for the other shoe to drop. *Waiting for the other shoe to drop* was one of the first idioms I learned in my English classes, and it had always sounded so ominous. I imagined slow, ghostly footsteps coming down a hall, getting louder and louder, the shoes dropping and coming closer, until you couldn't avoid them. It turned out Anna and I could still find new ways to avoid each other, even when we were on different continents.

I had one bit of information on her that she didn't know I had, that I'd never brought up or even alluded to. It could've been because of the timing, which had been so close to my departure, or because I thought I'd use it as leverage at some point. Either way, I'd found out she was having an affair exactly two weeks before I left for Greece.

It was evening and I was in the basement in my office. I picked up the phone to make a call and heard another person's voice. I was about to hang up, but realized that the voice belonged to a man, someone I didn't recognize. I paused for a second. Held my breath. No one noticed that I was on the other line.

"I miss you," the man's voice said. "I didn't see you all day."

"Let's have breakfast tomorrow," Anna said. "Early."

"Breakfast?"

"Hey, it's better than nothing." She laughed. No, she giggled. A low, honeyed peal.

"Okay, fine. Goodnight, sweetheart."

"Goodnight," Anna said, and then the phone clicked and I hung up, too.

I tried to place the voice. A co-worker? I didn't know any of them. Had she called him or did he call her? I thought I'd heard the phone ring, so I picked up the receiver again and traced the call. A monotone robotic voice recited a number, which I scribbled down on some paperwork. I didn't recognize it, nor did I call it back right away.

I could've handled the moment differently. I could've stormed upstairs and screamed, but instead I did nothing. I stayed in the basement until after Anna had fallen asleep, and when I went to bed, we didn't touch.

I spent the next few days playing detective. The number belonged to a man named Daniel who, I learned, worked with Anna. I drove by his house twice. It was nice, nicer than ours, and the cars in the driveway were nicer than ours, too. I parked and walked up to the house, peeked into the backyard quickly before anyone saw me. There was a pink bicycle and a half-deflated beach ball. Daniel had children, too.

After that phone call, I kept trying to answer the phone first just in case he called again, but they weren't that sloppy. A boy called once, though, for Zoe. This was new. He sounded shy. I was getting good at eavesdropping, so I waited before hanging up.

"Dad," Zoe said. "I got it. You can hang up now." She'd started calling me Dad in front of people, even though at home I was still Daddy. When I left, it would be Dad all the time.

"Will you leave me when I go to Greece?" I asked Anna a few days after driving by Daniel's house for the second time.

"I think you're the one technically leaving me."

"Anna."

"What?"

"I need to know."

She didn't say anything at first. She was thinking, probably, of him, Daniel. I wondered where they'd had sex.

"I won't leave you," she said. "Will you leave me?"

"No." I think in that moment we were both telling the truth. Despite everything, she was mine. We belonged to each other. That night we made love for the last time before I got on the plane.

I thought I would bring Daniel up when it made sense, but now that I'd had the perfect chance I'd faltered. I had to get out of my apartment. I walked to Pet Corner and Larissa looked happy to see me. At least I still had that. I didn't stay long, though. She was busy and promised to come over when the store was closed for the night. I fell asleep waiting for her, and when I woke up at midnight realized she wasn't coming.

I dropped by again the following evening, and she apologized—there had been a minor emergency with the owner, and she'd had to stay late. Tonight would be fine.

"Maybe I should wait outside until you're done." Instead of it sounding like a joke, it came out like a threat.

"Don't worry," she said. "I'll be there."

She arrived after 10 p.m., while I was sitting at my desk debating whether I should call.

"Is something wrong?" I asked when she pulled away from my embrace.

"Yes."

"What is it?"

"I'm going to have to stop seeing you."

"Why?"

"I have to get on with my life."

"What do you mean?"

"I'm getting married."

"Married? You?"

"Yes."

"This is news."

"You're not the only one with another life. I have a fiancé. He's coming this summer."

"Why didn't you tell me sooner?"

"I wasn't sure if he was really going to come."

"Where are you going to live?"

"We're moving into a bigger apartment with my sister and her husband."

"That sounds cramped." She just stared at me. "Does he know about me?"

"Of course not. My sister won't say anything."

"Why did he take so long?"

"He couldn't just pick up and leave."

"Let me marry you. We can move to Canada."

I could take her with me, buy a new house. Zoe could live with us, and she would like Larissa once she got over the strangeness of it. Anna would probably hate me, but she had Daniel. We could handle it, each of us.

"You know you would never do that. It's ridiculous."

"It's not." My voice caught as I explained the logistics to her. I was going to cry. *Crying*. It was embarrassing.

"Can I still visit you at the store?" I asked.

"You should go back to your family."

She left that night, but visited two more times in the following week, each time saying she wouldn't return, that it was over. I never believed her, but then a week passed, and another, and she didn't show up. Finally I made myself walk past Pet Corner so that I could talk to her, but she'd already closed up. The store was dark, and even the rabbits were asleep, so I returned home, alone.

ZOE

Peter and I woke up early the next morning. The musty smell of every cigarette ever smoked in that room had woven into the fibres of the sheets and the curtains and, overnight, had worked its way into my own pores and hair. In the shower, I was convinced that the water was infused with liquid smoke. We got ready quickly and hopped back into the car. We went through a McDonald's drive-through and bought coffee, hash browns, sausage Egg McMuffins. I unwrapped a McMuffin on my lap, put a squirt of ketchup on it and handed it to Peter to eat as he drove. He didn't want his coffee, so I drank both and fiddled with the radio dial, catching snippets of religious shows or sermons.

"This is what I imagined America would be like," I said to him.

"What do you mean?"

"McDonald's, a big car, Christian radio."

American highways were bigger, too, and better integrated into the landscape. Often we were surrounded by trees on both sides. Ancient, leafy brush snaked up around poles that lined the roads.

The temperature, going north, kept dropping, and the amount of snow crept higher as we approached Niagara Falls, like were we travelling back in time, leaving behind those brief days of spring in New York City and retreating back into winter.

We stopped at a diner in a small town for lunch. They had fudge for sale, blocks of it on display in a glass case by the cash register. Peter bought a chunk of rocky road, choco-latey and studded with rounds of marshmallows and nuts. It had a waxy bulk to it, like it was a precious metal, and we treasured it similarly. We got back in the car and explored the town, looking for the right place to eat our dessert. We ended up on a rural road that led toward a lake. It was still frozen over, and we decided to eat the fudge on the lake and then continue on our way.

There's something about walking on ice. A feeling, a kind of tingle, a spreading sensation in your thighs, like when you're up really high or when you're on a roller coaster, about to make that first drop. Eventually you relax and walk normally, less gingerly, but it still feels funny, conceptually, walking on water.

We walked further onto the lake and then Peter said, "Oh shit," and I saw him, waist-deep in snow. No wait, not snow. Water? The lake. Shit. It had happened so fast. Did I try to reach over and grab him? I don't remember, because then my legs were in the water, too. I grabbed at some ice and it dissolved like sand through my fingers. I tried again and this time it stayed solid and, like a seal, I pulled myself out belly first, face down, nose skimming the ice.

The tips of Peter's shoes were in my face. "It's okay," he said. "You can get up. It's solid here."

We turned around and shuffled back holding hands, afraid that one wrong step would cause the entire lake to crack open and swallow us whole. Once on shore we ran, our legs and torsos wet and heavy, and quickly changed. From the car, our footsteps made a muddled line down the middle of the lake toward the horizon. We should've known it was too warm for the ice to be walkable. There were certain spots where the snow had blown away, and the map of cracks in the ice looked so obviously dangerous, but we were, dumb city kids, and hadn't noticed.

We laughed at how things had gone wrong, but then fixed themselves so quickly. How if things had stayed wrong, it would've taken days for people to find us—no one knew where we were and who would've guessed that we'd be buying fudge in a small town in New York? For a second it was the funniest thing in the world.

Once, after I'd fallen off my bike and scraped up my knees and wrists, my father told me a trick to avoid accidents. The key was to think of time in its most basic elements, a long chain of seconds and nanoseconds lined up in a row, individual units that could be taken apart and examined. Chopped up. If you could chop time, you could slow it down, and when it was slow, you could arrange yourself to avoid mishaps, like the way cats right themselves mid-fall and land on their feet. What he didn't explain was how to do this when you're actually in the midst of experiencing the accident, and even he hadn't been able to follow his own advice.

"That was intense," Peter said. We'd stopped at the first coffee shop to warm up. We'd lost the fudge during the whole ordeal, so I was eating a doughnut.

"Yeah." My desire to talk about the lake was waning, the rush replaced with a delayed fear.

"We should do something to celebrate," Peter suggested.

"What are we celebrating? That we didn't die?"

"Yes. There are casinos at Niagara Falls; we're on a lucky streak."

"I don't want to gamble. What else do people do in Niagara Falls?"

"They go on honeymoons."

"So let's get married."

Peter laughed. "We've only known each other for three days."

"Technically we've known each other for years."

"True."

We got back in the car and kept talking about getting married. The idea appealed to me, and doing it quickly was even better. It was stupid, but why not? How well do you ever know a person, anyway? In the past few days Peter and I had walked blocks and blocks together, driven for miles, had sex in a motel and fallen into a lake. Big things, small things. If marriage was a commitment and we wanted to make that commitment, our focus and motivation could carry us forward.

My decision to visit Peter had been on the spur of the moment and ended up being the best decision I could've made; like he'd said, we were on a lucky streak. I could transfer schools and move to New York; we wouldn't stay in New Jersey, obviously. Emily could come visit. My mother would like Peter. His blond hair. She used to say we had too much brunette in our family, all of us with dark hair and brown eyes, like it was a curse. My parents knew each other for just under a year when they got married. My mother would understand if I married under the same circumstances.

"Will there be an official proposal?" I asked Peter.

"Will you marry me?" he asked. "I'm sorry I don't have a ring."

"It's okay. We've been through a lot already."

"Totally." Peter was grinning. "I love you."

"Okay," I said, trying it out. "I love you too."

"So we'll do it?"

"Yes."

"Niagara Falls must be important in my life, then," he said. "I was conceived there, and I'll get married there."

We kissed, and my chest hurt in a good way. Peter honked the horn.

I was never the kind of girl who dreamed about weddings and princess dresses and sugary cakes. Even with Hugo, I never saw us getting married. I pictured us with something beyond marriage, a deep, bottomless commitment, like getting matching tattoos instead of rings. Maybe I was more traditional than that. Maybe I'd never thought about marriage with Hugo because I knew, deep down, he'd never want to marry me.

For only a day in the car, we'd made a mess, our McDonald's cups, a smudge of doughnut icing on the passenger seat, a bag of Skittles on the dashboard. Our wet clothes in the back seat had dried into stiff folds and replaced the previous musty grandfather smell of the car with something lake-y, organic. The monkey head had fallen on the floor, so I picked it up and positioned it facing out the front window toward whatever came next. Our future, I guess.

My memories of Niagara Falls were in Canada in the summer when the city felt like an amusement park, all theme restaurants and packed tour buses. Niagara Falls, New York, with its piles of dirty, half-melted snow and empty storefronts, was bleaker. Our plan was to find a place to stay for the night and then figure out the wedding thing. Peter and I had started calling it that, "the wedding thing," like it was an object to acquire. I suppose it was—our custom-made souvenir commemorating our first trip together.

Most of the motels along the strip on Niagara Falls Boulevard had signs that said *SEE YOU NEXT SUMMER*, some missing letters, as if they'd been closed for longer than just the past winter season. We pulled into the lot of the Moonlite Motel. Its neon vacancy sign blinked on and off and the pool out front was covered with a tarp that had a shallow puddle of melted snow in its sagging centre. Neither of us got out of the car.

"It looks like the kind of place you bring someone to murder them," I said.

"I bet my parents had sex in Niagara Falls to stop from killing themselves."

"We don't have to stay here—we can go to the Canadian side for the night. We'll have to cross the border at some point anyway."

"Maybe," Peter replied, and drove past the remaining motels. There were signs directing us to the Falls, so we followed those. When we were close, a man wearing a parka and holding fluorescent orange flags waved us into an empty parking lot.

Peter unrolled the window. "Where is everyone?"

The man shrugged. "It's not exactly peak season right now. It's busier on the weekends."

"How much to park?"

"Ten dollars. You can also park for free across the street, by the curb. Two hours max, but they won't come by for a while."

We thanked him and found the spots. There were a few other cars, and in the distance someone was walking a pair of dogs, but otherwise the area was emptier than we'd expected.

To get to the Falls, we walked along a path along the gushing, brown Niagara River. It was stronger than any other river I'd ever seen. Rising mist froze in tiny droplets, encasing bare branches in the thinnest shells of ice. They were so delicate that when I reached up and touched one, the ice melted off immediately.

Finally the river dropped down into the Falls. I wasn't used to viewing them from this angle, behind them instead of head-on.

"What do you think?" I asked.

"I wasn't sure if they would impress me, but they do."

We leaned against the railing on our tiptoes for a better look until our feet got cold and then returned to the car and crossed the border at the Peace Bridge. A guard waved us through after glancing at our passports. We'd been nervous about it and they didn't even ask any questions.

The tackiness of Niagara Falls, Ontario, was comforting compared with the stony loneliness of New York. Up until this point I'd been more comfortable in empty, quiet areas—on buses, in the Empire State Plaza in Albany, in tucked-away corners of museums—but now with the wedding thing, I needed something louder. I would've married Peter in the middle of Times Square if we were still in New York City.

There were some motels hidden among the chains, and we stopped at the first one we passed.

"What brings you here?" the man at the desk asked us.

"A wedding," Peter said.

"Oh?"

"Ours, actually."

I blushed—something about a stranger knowing—but the man smiled. "You'll need the honeymoon suite, then. Not sure if the heat's on."

We stayed a step behind him as he led us to the room. From the back he had the most wrinkled and creased neck

I'd ever seen. Dark brown, like it had been isolated in a tanning salon. It didn't match the rest of his body.

He unlocked the door and bent over the radiator. "We have an indoor pool, but I keep that warm all the time. I hope you brought your bathing suits."

The room was small, with a circle-shaped bed and a heart-shaped Jacuzzi, which, I suppose, was what made it the honeymoon suite.

He straightened up. "It will take a few minutes for the heat to kick in, but I'm sure you know how to keep each other warm. Congratulations, kiddos!"

I locked the door behind him as soon as he left.

"What next?" I asked. It was early evening, so we'd have to do the wedding thing in the morning. I was relieved when Peter suggested we go to bed early.

The frozen lake felt so long ago now; so much had changed in a day. We needed to rest before tackling the rest of our lives.

ANNA

Zoe and I stayed with George and Katerina and their two children for Niko's funeral. George was so wonderful to us, and strong, and I tried to mimic him. He cried at the airport when he picked us up, and then again at the funeral, but not at any other point during our stay, although I would sometimes notice his face darken. At the arrival gate in Athens, I was struck by how much he'd aged: grey hair, wrinkles. We hugged each other. When we separated, he lifted his hand to his face and I thought it was to scratch his cheek, but then his hand had stayed there, and he looked away, and I saw his back heave up and down from a sob.

George took time off work and came with me to meetings at the police station, hospital and various government offices. I would be silent the entire time except for the initial condolences. They would tell me *I'm sorry* in English, their *r*'s rolled and guttural, and then proceed in Greek with George. Sometimes George would translate, sometimes he wouldn't. The man Niko had rented the boat from was old and poor. He didn't have insurance—he'd taken Niko's money without a receipt. Were we going to sue? No.

Athens was harder and rougher than when I was there for our honeymoon. There was constant traffic, and the streets were so much dirtier than I remembered. The first two days, I lay in bed awake for hours until falling asleep deeply. I'd wake up to Zoe staring at my face as if to make sure I was still alive.

I hadn't wanted Zoe to come to Greece, but of course she had to. I bought a black dress for her before we left, and then, when we arrived, realized I hadn't brought an entire black outfit for myself. Or matching blacks anyway. I had a shirt and a skirt, but the shirt had faded, and when I wore it with the skirt, the ensemble was frumpy and I was afraid the dowdiness was disrespectful. George took care of everything else so I suppose I had to be preoccupied with something.

Katerina drove me to a store not far from their home, and spoke to the saleswoman, who picked some dresses and handed them to me in a change room. *Efharisto*, I said to her, *thank you*, and it took so much energy to muster something in Greek that I didn't speak for the rest of my time at the store, just chose the first item that fit, let Katerina pay, and in the end the dress still fit poorly, but at least it was uniformly black and properly mournful.

It was also my job to clean out Niko's apartment. It was an empty, dusty, bachelor's apartment, and it didn't even have an extra room for Zoe if we'd visited. Niko hadn't thought to plan for more space, and I was angry instead of sad for the first time since the accident. I was pissed off that he'd embraced his new life so easily, accepted that Zoe and I weren't coming along.

I tackled the bedroom first on my own while Zoe sat on his balcony. The bedsheets were rumpled—Niko never made the bed in Canada, either. I gathered his things. Shirts, pants, some shorts.

"Do you want to send these back to Canada?" George had asked delicately.

"Can we donate them?" I couldn't imagine bringing everything back to Toronto, packing a suitcase without him there to carry it. George looked at me as if to say, *You don't donate a dead man's clothes*. So I threw everything into garbage bags. His clothes, shampoo, soap.

When Niko and I had first met, he'd told me that when he was no longer capable of changing his life, it would mean he was officially too old. I wasn't sure what he meant by "changing his life," but I was in my early twenties and it didn't seem like such a hard thing to do if you put your mind to it. At first, while rummaging through his things, it seemed like although he'd changed his life by moving to Athens, he'd more or less just transposed it. It didn't look too different, until I realized he'd had his share of secrets.

I found a box of condoms in his room. Opened. Next I found a woman's blouse, size small. It was folded carelessly with his clothes, as if he hadn't noticed washing it and putting it away. I hid these things quickly before Zoe walked in and then noticed a bracelet on the nightstand, a thin gold chain. When I found this third undeniable object, I leaned over and buried my head in Niko's pillow. It smelled like him a little, and mothballs, but nothing else. No one else. I held the pillow to my face until Zoe walked in.

"Someone's knocking at the door," she said. The knocks were loud, but I hadn't heard them. George had left to give us some privacy, so I got up and answered it. There were three people—an older couple and a younger woman. Did the blouse and bracelet belong to the younger woman?

"How can I help you?" I asked. "I'm sorry but I don't speak Greek."

"It's okay," the younger woman said. "My name is Valia. My parents, Maria and Spiro, wanted to talk to you. They live next door. I never met Niko, but they told me about him."

"You didn't know him?"

"I don't live in Athens. I'm just here to visit for a few days and I'd hoped I could finally meet him. We're all so sorry to hear what happened."

Maria was a big, soft woman, and she put her arms around my neck when her daughter stopped talking. "I'm sorry," she said in English, weeping. Spiro shook my hand solemnly, his eyes also brimming with tears. I had no idea who these people were.

Valia gave me a casserole dish. "My mother made you baklava. It was Niko's favourite."

Zoe hovered behind me. Maria leaned over and smothered her in a hug as well.

"Niko helped my parents take care of their turtle," Valia said.

"What turtle?" Zoe asked when she pulled away from Maria. Unlike me, she hadn't started crying.

"I can introduce you if you like."

I nodded to Zoe, and Valia took her hand and led her to their apartment. Of course she wanted to see the turtle. When Niko first moved, she'd seemed to have matured overnight. She was a teenager, a young woman, capable and independent. The accident had made her young again, though. We held hands often now as we navigated through Athens together; we hadn't done that in years.

Maria and Spiro remained in front of me. I tried not to cry again, but couldn't help it, and Maria hugged me tighter. I wanted Valia to come back so that I could ask her to ask her mother about what I'd found. She would know if Niko ever had visitors. If they were women.

But when Zoe returned with Valia, I didn't ask anything further and instead listened to her tell me about Spiro and Maria's turtle. Niko had helped them decorate its aquarium. It was such a peculiar story, one I hadn't expected, but I also hadn't expected him to have a mistress, and it appeared that he had.

When George came back, I had more or less composed myself. He could tell I wasn't doing well, though, and quickly helped us wrap up and return to his home. We were stuck in traffic for a while, and none of us spoke, although Zoe repeated the story of the turtle a second time, tickled by it.

That evening, George's wife made us dinner. We ate it on their balcony. Their children were out and Zoe had gone to bed early.

"It must have been hard today," George said to me when Katerina got up to clear the table. "Do you want to go back? I can take care of the rest."

"There's not much else to do. His apartment is a mess, though."

"Don't worry about cleaning it—we'll hire someone."

"I don't think he cleaned his bathtub once."

"I suppose he lived like a bachelor."

"From the state of his place, I'm assuming he rarely had guests over. Did you visit him a lot?"

"He usually came here, but he was very busy with work; he didn't have a lot of time to socialize."

"He was too busy for friends?"

"I think so."

"I'm not so sure about that."

"Why?"

"He probably had a few friends. Maybe he didn't want to introduce you." I scanned George's face for a reaction, and I'm positive that for a second he flinched. He didn't say anything, though. "That turtle, anyway. It's so bizarre. Niko hated animals."

"He was being nice to his neighbours."

"There's so much about his life here that I don't know."

"There was nothing important for you to know about. He missed you and Zoe. He asked me if he could break his lease so that the three of you could move to a larger apartment when you came to Athens."

"We were never going to move."

"Anna." George reached over and touched my hand. "It's terrible what happened. Of course you're angry."

"I'm not angry. I just wish I actually knew what happened. Before and after."

"The most important thing is that he loved you both." He got up. "I'm getting you another drink. You need one."

I wanted to show George what I'd found. The evidence. While he was gone, I took the bracelet out of my pocket, where I'd shoved it in a rush. His balcony was across the street from the sea, and I looked at it while I waited for him. When I heard him approach, I panicked and flung the bracelet away, aiming for the water. There's no way I'd thrown the bracelet into the sea, but it was better to think of it as washed away. Gone forever.

George had poured me a small cloudy glass of ouzo. I drank it quickly and went to bed that night with anise-scented breath.

Leading up to Niko's funeral, I worried that his mistress would come. There had been an announcement in the paper and the accident had been a minor news item—anyone could've seen it. In the end, Niko's funeral was small—his co-workers from Calypso (mostly male), his remaining family, me and Zoe. There was no mysterious woman hovering in the back behind a veil; I looked.

NIKO

I could pinpoint the moment when things started to feel like they were slowly unravelling to the day the washing machine broke. It was the beginning of a bad-luck phase. Another one. Not only was everything falling apart with both Anna and Larissa, but I was also back to working late at the office. Jimmy and Christos were preparing for a presentation to a potential American investor. They desperately needed a cash infusion, and were troubled by the numbers I presented to them, as if it was a genuine surprise that the company was doing poorly. I helped them with their pitch as much as I could, even though deep down we were doubtful we'd get much money from him.

Anna and I didn't continue the discussion we'd started about our problems. It wasn't so much that we avoided the topic, but that we avoided speaking, period. I spoke to only Zoe instead, not asking for Anna or her for me. One Saturday night, though, feeling lonely, I called them, hoping to talk to Anna as well for once. There was no answer. I couldn't remember if Zoe had said they were going anywhere, so I left a message asking them to call me back whenever they got home, even if it was late.

I thought about calling Larissa next and got as far as dialling most of the number. I hung up before finishing, and as soon as I did, a phone rang in another apartment. The buildings were so close together that it took me a moment to register that it wasn't coming from mine.

When I got to work on Monday, instead of taking the elevator to my office on the seventh floor, I took the stairs. The only other time I'd done this was on my second day at Calypso, four months ago now, when the elevators had been temporarily closed for maintenance. As my new co-workers and I made our way up, I'd told them about how once a year at my old job in Toronto, we would climb to the top of our thirty-story building for charity, for fun, and they'd looked at me like I was crazy. Jimmy had taken one look at the stairs, turned around and said he'd return when the elevators were operating, and I didn't see him again until the next day.

This Monday morning I walked for the simple desire to make myself feel worse than I already did. Why not push it even further? I was strong after the third flight and tired after the fourth, but I wasn't out of breath. When I arrived at my desk I was sweaty and breathing quickly, but the point was that I was breathing, period. That was good. All weekend I'd felt sunk underwater, like I couldn't move. At least now I knew I was alive, like that day I'd jumped into the sea from Jimmy's boat. I sat down heavily in my chair and a drop of sweat trickled down my back underneath my shirt.

Jimmy appeared at the door. "You look like hell."

"Thanks."

"Are you sick?"

"Bad weekend."

I'd slept about six hours combined on Friday and Saturday nights. On Sunday, knowing I had to be at the office in the morning, I'd forced myself to lie in bed and tried slowing down my thoughts. At 3 a.m. I gave up. I got dressed, put my shoes on and thought about taking a walk, but instead of leaving the apartment, went out onto the balcony and leaned against the railing. Every so often a taxi rounded the corner and then disappeared, momentary points of light. The top of a head and then a pair of heads made their way down the street, but no one else gave off signs of being awake. Athens was usually brimming with sounds, but there was a two-hour window in the middle of the night when everything was silent, when single noises reverberated like church bells if you were awake to hear them. I stood there, listening.

"Go home," Jimmy told me. He said it kindly. "Get some sleep."

I didn't protest. My shirt was now uncomfortably damp, and once he left, I got up. I took the elevator down to the lobby this time.

Instead of walking back to the subway station, I turned the other way and headed toward the sea. Calypso's offices were only a few blocks away from the passenger port in Piraeus, and I'd often walk over at lunch to check out the action. This, the early days of summer, was the busiest I'd seen it. Most people were with their families, everyone optimistically dressed in minimal clothing, luggage dropped at their feet. You could tell who was Greek by their olive skin, and even if they weren't tanned, they were the ones holding plastic cups of frappés and chewing on straws. The other tourists were pale or pink, knobby-kneed. An old man pushed a cart of bread and sugared doughnuts, while another waved around a stick strung with lottery tickets. Some Pakistani immigrants were hawking fake designer sunglasses and cheap, useless knick-knacks.

Scattered around the port, men sat inside kiosks and shouted out names of the islands their boats sailed to. People assume that because I was born in Greece, I'm familiar with its islands, but I haven't set foot on most of them. Santorini, Mykonos, Crete, Rhodes. The big tourist islands. I could visualize them, but I'd never been.

I approached a kiosk for a boat to Spetses. It left in an hour and then again later, at six.

"Do you still have tickets for the later boat?" I asked.

"One-way or return?"

"Return."

"When are you coming back?"

"I'm not sure."

"You can decide when you get there, then." He sold me a one-way ticket, and while it would've been cheaper to buy a round trip, I wasn't in the mood to negotiate.

At home I packed. I hadn't unpacked completely from the trip to Meteora and when I emptied my bag out on my bed, discovered that I'd accidentally taken one of Larissa's shirts. It was silky and soft. It had been two weeks since I'd last seen her; I could use the shirt as an excuse to contact her, maybe. I folded it and put it away in my dresser. I wasn't going to call her, or anyone else now, anyway. Later.

Only Flying Dolphins went to Spetses. I took a window seat and expected to fall asleep immediately, but looked outside the entire trip instead. The Flying Dolphin navigated out of the port slowly and then picked up speed. When we were further out, I saw large ships in the water, stationary. They didn't have the proper permits to dock in Athens in Keratsini Bay so they sat there, sometimes for days, until it was possible to come in. None belonged to Calypso.

The sea was calm for the first hour, and then the wind got stronger and the waves choppier. The water darkened to a deep navy blue. The waves looked like they were made of something almost solid, liquefied marble, shot through with veins of white and capped with frothing foam.

As the sun set, the sky turned pink and then purple and grey. It remained in this dusky haze for a good portion of the trip, and when I looked further out, I couldn't distinguish between land and sea. They melted into each other. I saw small, jagged outlines of islands, and when the Flying Dolphin approached them, I could tell they were mainly uninhabited, just rocks and shrubs. Lights on fishing boats bobbed up and down in the rough waves around us.

I wasn't sure why I'd chosen to go to Spetses. It was familiar, but not too familiar, I suppose. Even though my father had been born on the island, I didn't have any family there anymore. He'd lived in Spetses for only three years before they moved to Piraeus for KML, and when I was growing up we didn't visit often, only sometimes in August to get away from the city.

Anna and I had gone to Spetses on our honeymoon, although we'd visited my parents in Athens first. They were strong then and still worked on their writing projects. They loved Anna. My mother kept telling me how pretty she was, as if she was surprised by it. I'd wanted to hoard her all to myself, and I'd felt like I was doing just that when I'd swept her away in the ferry toward Spetses. She'd gotten so tan that after only the first few hours she had tan lines from her bathing suit on her naked body.

But I wasn't going to Spetses because of Anna, or because of my family. I was going because it was a good place to catch my breath, and, as I'd reminded myself that morning, I needed to breathe. It was maybe foolish to take a last-minute vacation. I could've waited, made sure there wasn't anything pressing to do at work. But sometimes you did things without thinking through the consequences, and they turned out fine. Not always, but usually. I'd done something impulsive, but I could've done worse.

It took two attempts for the captain to dock in Spetses, but once I was off the boat I couldn't tell the water had been rough. It was dark out and the area surrounding the harbour glowed with streetlights. I bypassed the hotels that promised seaside views and took a narrow, dimly lit path toward rooms that would be cheaper and quieter. Around a corner I found a small pension called Villa Christina. The front door opened up into a leafy courtyard, and two women sat at a table lit by candlelight, engrossed in conversation. One of them smoked a pipe.

"Good evening," a man called from a balcony above. "How can I help you?"

"Do you have any rooms?"

"For how long?"

"A few days."

He came down with a set of keys and showed me a room with a double bed, a television hanging in the corner and two glass doors opening up to a small balcony. I paid him a deposit in cash, and when he left I kicked off my shoes. The tiled floor was cool beneath my feet. The bed was hard, but it was good to stretch out on clean sheets, and I slept better than I had in weeks.

I woke up with the sun streaming through the window and onto my face. My back was stiff and I was starving from not having eaten much the day before. I groaned a low, pathetic rumble. Groaning was better than crying, though. I wondered what the woman with the pipe would think if she heard me.

I found my phone and called the office. The secretary, Barbara, answered. "I hear you're sick," she said, clucking. I was fairly certain Jimmy was sleeping with her. "You shouldn't have come in yesterday."

"I am sick," I lied. "Can I talk to Jimmy?"

"He won't be in until after lunch."

"I'm going to need a few days off to recover." I was relieved that I'd missed him, even if he would be the first person to understand a last-minute island vacation.

"No problem. I'll tell him. Take care of yourself."

I got dressed and made my way toward a clump of cafés I'd seen the night before. I looked for something familiar. The most definitive memories I had of Spetses were the few days I spent with Anna, but it was a different island then, not as developed, not as popular. Now, especially in the main town, it was more like a rich seaside suburb of Athens than a separate piece of land—more men in fashionable white pants, fewer fishermen.

I continued past the main town and wove past houses and churches. Cars weren't allowed on the island, and although motorbikes clogged the main town, I didn't encounter any here. Everything was still. The streets were lined with lemon trees laden with fruit or big swatches of fig trees sprouting close to the ground. I poked around one and found figs hidden within the broad leaves, tight green closed fists. They wouldn't be ready to eat until August, but I pulled two off anyway and rolled them between my palms. I understood why older men fiddled with worry beads, how the feeling of something smooth in your hands could be comforting.

I arrived on the older part of the island where people kept sailboats. There were fishing boats, too, dozens crammed together in the port, their bumpers knocking against each other. Some sailboats were especially beautiful, gleaming wood and double masts with ropes and sails stretching high up in the air. I threw the figs in the water. Maybe what I needed was a boat of my own.

I stopped at one of the handful of seafood restaurants along the shore and sat at a table on a small dock, and through the wooden slats the sea sloshed against the sand. I ordered a beer and a plate of small fried fish, the kind you eat head, tail and all. While I was waiting, someone from the kitchen came out and tossed a handful of leftover bread into the sea. The pieces bobbed at the surface and then small ripples formed around them. I looked closer and saw fish, a swarm of them, nipping at the soggy bread. My lunch?

"Do you know where I can rent a boat?" I asked when the man returned with my food. He turned out to be the owner of the restaurant.

"There are some travel agencies in town, but they're expensive."

I could tell he was baiting me. "Do you have a better deal?"

"I don't, but my friend Costa has some boats. He's a fisherman. He'll be here soon; I'll introduce you."

When I finished my meal, Costa came by my table. He was an older man with white hair and the swollen, callused hands of someone who's relied on them for most of his life. He smelled, too, slightly sour, but this made me trust him—he was someone who actually worked with boats.

"You're a sailor?" he asked me.

"Not exactly."

"Where are you from?"

"Athens, but my father was from Spetses. My family was in shipping—they started off here."

I could tell this pleased him. "So you must know how to sail a boat?"

"I've lived in Canada for the past twenty-five years. I haven't been out on the water for a while."

"Where in Canada?"

"Toronto."

"I have a cousin in Vancouver. I've never been; I'm too busy here."

"Do you know where I can rent a sailboat?"

"For yourself?"

"Yes."

"Alone?"

"Yes."

He looked at me, amused. "No one will trust a Canadian who hasn't lived by the sea in twenty-five years alone with their sailboat, but if you want to rent a motorboat, I can help you out. I have a few. You can go fishing."

A motorboat was less enticing, but admittedly a sailboat was daunting. A motorboat was simple—you turned it on, you pointed the rudder, you went on your way. All I really wanted to do was get out on the water and clear my head. It didn't matter what vessel I used. I could even catch a few fish. My room at Villa Christina had a kitchenette, and I'd seen a small frying pan. I could make myself a meal.

Costa and I agreed to meet at the restaurant the next morning to sort it out. The restaurant owner was probably getting a kickback, but at least I didn't have to do any more work. One of the first things I'd loved about America was how straightforward it was. You didn't haggle over prices, and if you had to get a bureaucratic task done, you just showed up at the appointed office and waited for a while, but not so long that it would've made more sense to send your grandmother in your place because you couldn't afford to waste an entire day in line. I'd managed to secure a boat while drinking a beer—that felt like competence. The last time I'd done something so smoothly was when I'd ordered the rock for Bouboulina's aquarium.

I was reminded of Maria and Spiro's turtle—the reason I met Larissa in the first place—often in Spetses. Bouboulina, the human, had died here, and her statue stood in a square by the water, her pupils painted on the bronze, a shock of white compared to the tarnished metal. Her hand shields her eyes as she looks out toward the sea, pensively but defiantly. The statue was a popular meeting place, and kids climbed up and wrapped their arms around her waist, while others imitated her stance for photos.

Her house had been converted into a museum. I went on a guided tour of it that afternoon after meeting Costa. It was an elegant, neo-classical building more typical of a plantation in the southern United States than, Greece, and it was full of artifacts from all over the world: her wedding chest lined with tapestries, a decree from the czar of Russia giving her diplomatic immunity, a painting of her standing straight up in a boat, the men around her cowering in fear as she directed them toward the armed walls of Nafplio. The painting had been based on a real incident, which had been a brave moment for her, but a stupid one for the others—everyone, except her, was killed.

To die spectacularly, to go out in a heroic, terrific blaze, is a privilege. It might be an immature way of thinking, but stories of inconsequential expirations depressed me. One minute you're there and the next you're gone, no proper bridge in between, or if there is one, flimsy. For all the drama and intrigue of Bouboulina's life, her death was small. She was shot in the head in the dark, with no chance to defend herself. It wasn't even because of any noble cause for her country, but because her son had eloped with the daughter of another family in Spetses, one she didn't like. She was used to guiding her country to freedom, and it must have been frustrating that she couldn't wield that power to direct her son's love to a more worthy candidate. She went to their house to complain and ended up dead. I always wondered if the person who shot her truly meant to kill her or if they were just trying to scare her. They might have aimed for the shoulder and gotten the head instead.

I also still remembered how my mother's poem about Bouboulina ended:

We're watching, Bouboulina, but watch out too.
Be careful.
You have a lifetime ahead of you.
And when you don't,
We'll rejoice in the one you left behind.
We'll remember.

When I met Costa again, he was smoking with the owner of the restaurant. "Welcome, sailor!" he called.

He led me to the harbour and pointed to the cluster of boats that belonged to him. There was a more modern motorboat, but there were also a few skiffs, wooden and painted white with red trimming, their insides a pale blue, different shades depending on when they'd last been painted. The motorboat was bigger, sturdier, but I liked the look of the fishing boats, what I thought real fishermen like Costa used when they caught fish. One of them had a short mast so that you could raise a sail if you wanted to cut the outboard motor for a while. The name on the side was *Eleni*.

"I want that one," I said, pointing to it. "Why *Eleni*?"

"It's named after my youngest daughter: small, but strong. Are you sure you don't want the motorboat?"

I nodded my head. We negotiated the price briefly, mostly so that I could assert myself, not because I thought the price was unfair. I agreed to rent it until the end of the week. After I'd paid him, he showed me around: the motor, the rudder, the radio. It was simple, and I was grateful that I hadn't gone to the trouble of chartering an entire sailboat I wouldn't have known how to handle.

"It's windy these days," he said. "Make sure to check the weather before going out. The morning and early afternoon are best. Later than that and the meltemi comes in."

"Meltemi?"

"The strong winds from the Aegean. They start in May; good for the heat, but bad for boats."

There was an entire vocabulary related to the sea that I didn't know, but pretended to. "Of course," I said.

Costa gave me the keys and helped me untie the boat. I stepped in, turned on the motor, waved goodbye and, before I lost my nerve, puttered out into the sea for my first ride.

I'd imagined myself sitting on empty waters, just me, my small boat, the sea and sky above me, but I'd discounted how close I was to land. Even after the harbour was well behind me, I was surrounded. Mainland was close, just a short ride away, and there were other nearby islands, too. The closest was an islet, Spetsopoula, which was owned by the Niarchos family. I could jump out of the boat and, in whichever direction I swam, I would arrive at shore without much effort. And there were other boats, too, some motorboats, sailboats of varying sizes. We would wave at each other when we were close. I relaxed.

Costa had lent me a fishing rod and line, but I didn't feel like catching fish right away. I just wanted to be in the water. I raised the sail and felt the wind push me forward. It was good to come out here, to form new memories, to learn things that I should've learned as a child. Being on the island calmed me. The next time I came out I would pack some food and beer, drop anchor and eat and swim in the deepest waters, alone, by choice.

ZOE

We arrived at City Hall when it opened, but a lineup of people had already formed where we were supposed to pick up the marriage licence. While I saved our spot in line, Peter went out to get coffee and bagels. We'd been so excited when we'd woken up that we hadn't bothered getting breakfast. I gave him Canadian money and when he handed back the change, he dragged out the *oohs* in the words *loonies* and *toonies*.

We were still eating our bagels when it was our turn at the booth.

"One marriage licence, please," Peter said.

The woman handed over a form. "You have to be eighteen for a licence."

"We are." He had cream cheese on the corner of his mouth.

The form wasn't very complicated: our names, addresses, our parents' names, birthdays. Peter picked up the pen chained to the counter and started filling it out.

"What do we do when we get the licence?" I asked.

"What do you mean?"

"Where do we go to get married?"

"We don't do drive-through weddings here."

"So, where do people get married?"

"Um, anywhere. You can get a judge or clergyman or a justice of the peace, but we don't hold ceremonies at this City Hall. It's your responsibility to find a place, and witnesses too. The licence is valid up to ninety days. Do you want it or not?"

It cost a hundred dollars, which sounded like a lot of money for something that wouldn't immediately result in a wedding thing.

"We'll come back tomorrow." I folded the application and put it in my bag.

"That was weird," Peter said when we got back to the car.

"Yeah, she wasn't very helpful."

Without the licence, we weren't sure what to do anymore. It was supposed to have moulded the rest of the day.

We drove down to the main strip, which even at this time of year was busier and more alive than across the border. Outside the Guinness Book of World Records Museum, a fibreglass replica of the World's Tallest Man stood at the entrance. I came up to his waist.

"I can't believe neither of us brought a camera," Peter said.

In my rush to pack when I'd left Montreal, I hadn't thought to bring mine. I rarely took photographs, though. I relied on my writing to remember events, but Peter was right, we needed one. I wanted to record this, the way we looked, the way he looked, and words weren't enough. My favourite pictures of my parents are the ones from when they were first married. Their honeymoon in Greece. I had one of them in Spetses, tanned and young and beautiful. Everything had changed after that picture was taken, but at that moment their lives had looked impossibly perfect.

We found a place that took pictures that made it look like you were in a barrel going over the Falls. The lineup was longer than at City Hall, but it was better than nothing. While we waited we read a placard about Roger Woodward, one of the few people to have ever survived the plunge without any form of protection—just a bathing suit and a life jacket. He was seven years old. His sister, Deanna, was fished out just before going over, but everyone else on their capsized boat died. While Roger was in the water, he made peace with the fact that he was going to die, and he thought he was dead when they reeled him in.

Peter leaned in toward a photograph of the rescued Roger, soaked and skinny as a wet cat. "We looked like that in the lake."

When it came time to take the pictures, we threw our hands up in the air and screamed. This fake terror was fun compared to what I'd felt at the lake. "Ahhhh!" I screamed again, longer and louder than Peter. In two of the three shots, my eyes are closed, but I look happy.

At the end of the strip were the Falls. We'd meant to save them until the wedding thing worked out, but they were right there and we didn't have a good reason to avoid them. As we walked toward the groups of tourists in the viewing area, I noticed the entrance to the *Maid of the Mist*, the boat ride that takes you practically under the Falls. It was closed for the season, but the path heading down toward the water where you board the boat was still accessible, just barred by a gate low enough to hop over. We hopped.

At the bottom, we were as close as we could get to the Falls without leaving dry land. They were more amazing up close, white and gushing, more impressive than what we'd seen in New York. Huge chunks of ice clogged the basin, but if you looked closely, you could see them shifting from the constant flow of water, slowly eroding until they would dissolve completely away in time for spring and summer.

The way I'd felt as a child when I'd been here with my

parents and George flooded back, like we were explorers who had stumbled onto something new. The water, for all of its wildness, was contained in its chute downward, only the scattering of mist hitting us like soft rain. The nylon of Peter's thin coat was wet, but not as bad as when we'd fallen into the lake—slick, but not soaked.

At the photo studio, we'd also learned that in the early 1900s, when people did dumber/braver things, when there weren't guardrails, they would walk straight into the basin of the Falls and hike along those big, flat pieces of ice to examine the chute up close. It had sounded stupidly dangerous, but from our vantage point the ice looked like it could be strong at the right time of year. A trip across was entirely possible. Not now—we'd learned our lesson from the lake—but when it was colder.

"Wow," Peter said.

I breathed in the sharp, cold air and searched for another word, something to better capture all of this, the Falls, the blocks of ice, the grey sky. Peter's cheeks were pink. I really did need a camera. We stayed there for a while, longer than we had on the other side.

A gust of wind made us shiver and, instead of turning around, we huddled closer together. Our jackets rubbed against each other, and I thought of animals hibernating in the winter, their extra pads of fat, their breathing slow and heartbeats quiet. I thought of how sleeping was their trick to collapse time, how when they woke up months later, everything was different, the days warmer and easier.

ANNA

I knew I shouldn't worry about Daniel, but over a half-hour had passed and he still wasn't back at the hotel. The cell-phone rang and I fished it out of my bag—was it him? Had he gotten lost?

"Hello?"

"Hey, Mom."

I sat back down on the bed. Zoe.

"Is everything okay?" she asked. "I have, like, a million missed calls from you."

"I don't think I called you that many times."

"I was worried something had happened."

"I just wanted to see how you were doing. Where are you?"

"Niagara Falls."

"Why Niagara Falls?"

"It's just a stop before going home."

"I feel like I'm missing something, Zoe."

"It will take too long to explain now, but I'm fine, everything is good. Promise. How's Paris?"

I sighed. I could push it or move on. "It's fine. The weather is good, too." What meaningless, airless comments. I thought about everything I'd wanted to tell her or ask her and had resorted to talking about the weather instead. Maybe she was right, it was too much to fit into a long-distance phone call. "I miss you," I said to her. "I'll be home in two days. Come visit me."

"Maybe."

The phone beeped because it was running out of batteries, so we ended our call.

It was starting to get dark outside and I was officially worried about where Daniel had gone. I was looking out the window when I heard a knock at the door.

"What took you so long?" I asked when I saw him.

"I got lost," he said. "Did you take a nap?"

"Yes," I lied. "Kind of."

"The owner gave me a recommendation for dinner tonight—he wrote down the address."

I took the slip of paper, and it was the same restaurant he'd suggested to me earlier. He must have forgotten we were together.

"Should we go to that restaurant tonight?" I asked.

"I'm tired of thinking about the future. We're on vacation—let's decide when we're hungry."

I took this as confirmation that he'd been thinking about the things I was afraid he would be thinking about—the future, our future. I was tired of it, too.

We lay in bed. Daniel's body was always so warm. The rain had brought a dampness to the hotel that clung to the heavy drapes and sheets, and it was good to be near him, absorbing his heat. He smelled of the outdoors and also had a whiff of smoke on him, too, like he'd been at a bar.

"I'm glad you came back," I said.

"I almost didn't."

For a few minutes I thought he was sleeping, but then he spoke. "Are you happy with me?"

"Yes," I said, almost crying at the question. "Isn't it obvious?"

"No."

"Are you happy with me?"

"Sometimes."

"Only sometimes?"

"Usually. Is that better?"

"No."

"Tough luck."

On our last day in Paris, it was still drizzling outside.

"Don't tell me it's raining again," Daniel said from the bed. We'd had too much to drink the night before and were slow waking up.

"It is. Sorry."

We'd planned on going to the Musée des Egouts, dedicated solely to Paris's sewer system. We'd seen the sign for the museum, read about it in the guidebook and gotten curious. Afterwards we were going to visit Sacré-Coeur in Montmartre. Above and below, but below first.

"I'd rather see sewers than the catacombs," I said of the other place Daniel had suggested. "I don't want to see bones."

"You'd rather see shit than bones?"

"Today, yes."

The museum was surprisingly bustling. It was by the Seine, and as we descended a flight of stairs, the air cooled and smelled more septic—not unpleasant, just earthier. The cement walls were damp and every so often, a churned-up river of sewage gushed by behind grates. In one corridor gigantic steel spheres were on display. Sewer workers would push them through the pipes to squeeze out whatever didn't belong. The thought of these spheres coming loose in the museum and tipping down the narrow corridor we were walking through made me claustrophobic, aware that we were so close to water.

Daniel kept running excitedly ahead of me to see what

came next. Every time I caught a glimpse of him in the next room, I felt a swelling in my chest. I started purposefully walking slowly to test if the feeling would return, and it did, again and again.

When we emerged from the museum, the rain had stopped. The roads were still slick, and we wandered along the Seine, the smell of sewage stuck in my nostrils. On one of the bridges, I stopped and took the box with the ring out of my purse.

"I hope you're not going to throw it in the river," Daniel said.

"I was going to do the opposite." I opened the box, but he stopped me before I could take the ring out.

"Come on, Anna."

"What?"

"Not now."

"Why? I want to wear it; I've decided." My eyes welled up with tears, and I recalled how I felt on our first day when I couldn't pay my bill at the restaurant. Everything made me cry in Paris.

"I don't think now's the best time to rush into this."

"'Rushing' is the opposite of everything we've ever done together. We're not rushing into anything." These were arguments Daniel had given me in the past.

"We have too much to talk about. About us. About Niko. You've hardly said a word to me since I proposed."

"You haven't said much, either." I didn't mean it as a reproach, but it came out defensively.

"We're terrible."

"I should throw the ring away, then."

"Don't. I'll return it and get my money back instead."

"You're so sensible."

"Someone has to be."

I didn't know if I wanted to continue joking like this or be serious, so I put the ring away and we walked to the Métro to go to Montmartre.

"We can't split up in Paris," I said. "It's not allowed."

"Okay, but we're not getting engaged here, either."

"Fine. It would've been cheesy anyway."

I had visited Sacré-Coeur during my first trip. I was with Hélène that time, not Jean-François. I'd asked her about him, innocently, and she said they hadn't spoken since she'd introduced him to me the night I arrived. She shrugged her shoulders. *Men.* The steps to Sacré-Coeur were steep, and we'd bounded up them and at the top didn't speak of Jean-François again.

Daniel and I also walked up at a good clip and then joined the groups of people sitting on the top of the steps to catch our breath. The stretch of Paris below us was grey and white and matched the billowing creamy canopy of clouds above us. I counted church spires poking out above buildings until I lost track.

"It will be nice to be home," Daniel said. "Despite how beautiful this is."

"Can we talk about the ring when we get home?"

"Okay."

"I tried it on in the bathroom. It fits perfectly."

"Save it for home."

"Okay." I leaned into him.

We had one more night in Paris. We'd have dinner at a restaurant by Place des Vosges, and we'd order another bottle of wine. We would sleep deeply and then leave. Back at home we would be comfortable again. I would come clean, stop telling secrets. We would get married. Maybe. Probably.

For the longest time I'd felt something like a helium balloon, like I was only barely tethered to the Earth. I wanted to stop feeling like that. I wanted weighty proof of myself instead, and I could get it, or at least try, when I got home.

NIKO

I finally called Toronto that evening. Zoe answered. "Hi, Dad," she said. Chirpy, happy. "Have you been busy? I left a few messages at your apartment."

"I'm not home. I'm on an island, actually."

"Really? A vacation?"

"Kind of. Is your mother home?"

"Not yet. Do you want me to get her to call you later?"

"No, I'll talk to her when I'm back."

"Where are you anyway?"

"Oh, just a little island near Athens." I wasn't sure what Anna's reaction would be if she found out I was in Spetses, so I didn't tell Zoe in case she passed it on.

"Dad," Zoe said, her voice trailing off for a second. "It's weird that you and Mom never talk to each other anymore."

"What do you mean?"

"Is something wrong?"

I was surprised that Zoe had noticed, but maybe I shouldn't have been. Even if I thought of her as a little girl, she wasn't, and it probably wasn't too hard to pick up on the tension between Anna and myself. "It's difficult being in different countries sometimes," I said lamely, wanting to give her an explanation without having to reveal any details.

"When are you going to come back, then?"

"It's not that simple. Anyway, you two will visit me here." I ignored the fact that Anna had already suggested that Zoe come alone, without her. "As soon as we're together as a family, everything will be fine. I can't wait for you to come. Let's book the tickets when I'm back in Athens."

"Okay, Dad. Have fun."

I knew she wasn't convinced by my answers, but what could I tell her? I barely knew the answers myself. I remembered that when I was younger I always knew when my parents thought they were hiding something from me. If I suspected they had a secret, I would investigate until I discovered what it was, and it usually didn't take very long—some strategic eavesdropping, a pointed question or two. The only exception was when it came to their writing; I didn't push myself to get to the bottom of it. Even when I read their poems, it was as if an impermeable membrane blocked the true meaning of their words. Anna once suggested that perhaps, as their only son, I already knew the essential meaning of what they created.

My parents shared a writing desk in our apartment. I sometimes sat at the desk to study, but usually opted for the kitchen table instead; the desk was their domain. It was messy and cramped and the typewriter took up half the surface space. When my parents were too old to live on their own, I arranged for them to live in a senior citizens' home. It was a good place in a suburb far from Kypseli, a long bus ride away followed by a walk along a highway. To keep up the pretense that they might return to their apartment one day, we didn't sell it when they moved, so the desk was never properly cleared out until after both of them had died and I sold the apartment and realized it was my duty to sort through its contents. The desk itself, solid oak and heavy, was too cumbersome to ship to Canada and I didn't know anyone in Athens who needed it, so it was thrown out.

The surface was so raised with bumps from the pressure of thousands of pens and pencils that it was impossible to write on smoothly. You'd have to plane a good layer off the top for it to be usable again.

I sifted through its drawers and was left with a stack of notebooks—hardcover, softcover, some falling apart, some barely used. My mother typed her drafts and kept them in a series of blue cloth-covered folders held shut with elasticized white ribbons, while my father preferred to write with pencil on whatever scraps of paper were lying around. His pencils were more like crude tools, flattish wooden things that didn't fit into standard pencil sharpeners. He'd use a knife to shave away the surrounding wood when the tip was too dull to write with. He insisted on using these pencils until they were chewed up and stubby. I threw out dozens of them when I cleared out the apartment, not just from the desk, but various locations: the bedroom, the kitchen, two behind the fridge, one sitting with the toothbrushes in the bathroom. My mother used fountain pens, the cheap kind that leaked in sporadic, purple splotches across papers or her fingertips. She insisted on pressing down hard when she wrote, like she was trying to draw blood.

My father preferred to write in the morning and my mother at night, which was how they managed to share one workspace. I'd suggest they buy a second desk, but they appreciated the intermingling of their notes, and I'd often see my father's pencil marks on my mother's pages or the other way around.

I didn't prefer one parent's poetry to the other. It was the same to me, the product of the same desk, the same lexicon, the same well of experience. To be so entangled could be claustrophobic, but they thrived on it. They were never jealous of each other. When my mother got a poem published, my father would stand on a chair on the balcony and recite it to the street below. No one would hear him, but my mother would stand to the side and clap. When my father was published, my mother would clip out the poem and read it to herself, her eyes welling up with tears of pride. My father would smile and look at his words and say, "Not bad, not bad," as if he wasn't the person who had written them.

My father mainly wrote about water and my mother about land. Sometimes my mother wrote about the sea, or my father about the desert, and there were many poems about neither, but after paging through most of their work, even superficially, this pattern emerged. So many people look at the sea and think of a kind of hazy freedom, the vast stretch of possibilities. My father, rather than feel liberated by the image and the idea of the sea, felt constrained, but since it was in his blood, he couldn't escape it. At least, this was what I gathered from his poetry. My mother, on the other hand, was preoccupied with her position in the world, in the city, in her home, in her family. She often evoked trails and paths winding through varied lands, the journeys she, or someone else, took to arrive at their final resting place. It was starting to dawn on me that *The Solitary Woman*, which I'd been both proud of and embarrassed by, was about staking a claim in the world, even if she was entangled in other things, other people, other lives.

Her poems about the Graeae emphasized this the most. When I cleaned out the desk I was surprised to find variations of the poem she'd included in her book. The sisters spent their lives passing their shared single eye back and forth. Everything I'd learned about them was unpleasant—

they were ugly and petty; they had been born prematurely old and their long, grey-white hair was responsible for sea foam on a windy day. Despite this, people sometimes said their bodies had the shape of swans. My mother was generous to them in her poems.

> *We went swimming. I left everyone behind.*
> *Dove deep until I touched the sand*
> *and when I emerged, there were birds.*
> *Three of them, silver and long necked,*
> *their feathers ruffled by the waves.*
> *I swam closer. I waved.*
> *Only one looked. The other two,*
> *blind.*

She re-imagined our family as the trio, as if the three of us shared that one eye and saw everything filtered through that same lens. This was only true, though, when I was young, when my parents still had the power to herd me into their own little unit. All children are helpless, bound to their parents' eyes until they learn how to look beyond them to the rest of the world.

Anna used to accuse me of neglecting my parents as they got older. She had a more loving and friendly relationship with hers, and she saw them at least once a week until they died. My situation was different, though—we were in different countries and I couldn't take care of them with that much distance between us. While they weren't happy at first about being moved to the home, I'd had no choice. I wasn't neglecting them, just dealing with the situation, and although they rarely gave me the satisfaction of saying that they enjoyed it there, their nurses would tell me otherwise. George would also visit occasionally and assure me that they had friends and were well taken care of.

And besides, they had their poetry, their books. Books were more loyal companions than me, demanding so little, just a bit of time, which they had plenty of. Whenever I visited they would give me a list of books to find, and before I left they would have them to tide them over until I came again.

For all the frustrations I had with my parents, what distinguished them most from other people were their convictions. My father went out of his way to avoid steady work so that he could remain committed to his writing, and my mother never complained about it, never tried to convince him otherwise. She wrote her poetry when all the other mothers I knew perfected more domestic activities. I say that my uncle Alexander respected hard work, but I know my parents worked hard in their own way. They taught me how to be stubborn. That was worth something, for better or for worse.

Unfortunately, the magical powers they got from their writing and reading didn't stem the aging process. When their memories started to fail, I became paranoid about my own. I would wake Anna up in the middle of the night and ask her what we'd had for dinner a week ago because I wasn't sure if I remembered correctly. There were entire swaths of my life in Greece that seemed erased, wiped clean, so when I moved back, I was relieved that I remembered them again. Maybe memories aren't lost, but buried under layers of ash and stone, dust that can be cleared away in the right circumstances, like an archaeological dig. A few pieces might go missing, but the outline remains, waiting to be filled in again.

If my parents had continued living in their apartment until the end of their days, those scraps of papers, chewed-up pencils or marked-up books could've been the fuel they needed to remain themselves. If I did anything wrong, it was taking them away from their detritus.

After my parents died, I discovered poems in their desk that I'd never read before. My father had written one that started,

When the time comes,
fashion me a death mask of thin gold leaf.
Cover my face,
even if I'm smiling.

As my mother had gotten older, she'd written more about other people. Poets, like Cavafy, for instance. Rather than embrace the bohemian lifestyle of a poet, he'd worked as a civil servant until he retired, and even though he was gay, he lived with his mother until he died, and never with another man. His poems were concise and elegant and the restraint in them was so powerful it burned. That's what my mother said about him in her poems, anyway.

My parents' poems always confused me. They were painful in a way, like looking straight into the sun. While it was sometimes fascinating knowing what made my parents happy or sad, I'd be left with too many questions. Why were they moved to record certain events or write about certain people but not others? I'd wonder too much about the exclusions. For a long time I didn't think it was even appropriate for me to know this kind of information. Insight into their psychology—their messy fears and emotions—eroded the stability of their existence. I didn't want Zoe to have these kinds of questions about me. I didn't want to give her unfinished thoughts, a collection of random disappointments or joys. It's too much to know this about your parents. They're already in you—they made you. That my body had done its part in sequencing Zoe's DNA was knowledge, burden or constraint enough.

When I packed to go abroad for school, I almost left without a trace of my parents' poetry; however, with an end in sight, the apartment changed shape. Despite the heavy wood furniture, the old photos on the wall, the stacks of books, it looked less and less dreary. I brought *The Solitary Woman* with the simple white cover, the original Greek version and not the translation, and that's what I presented to others, including, eventually, Zoe. Even though I'd sometimes show it off, when I was asked to translate a poem, I said it was too complex. I wasn't lying: maybe it wasn't from a literary perspective, but for me, emotionally, it was.

My parents, sitting on the balcony and smoking. Reading from books out loud. I can remember certain lines of their poetry, but I mix their words up all the time. Our apartment was always dusty, except for the books, which would get moved around, picked up and carried from one room to another and left in the bathroom, on the balcony, on the bed. For a long time I was disgusted by this life. It was only natural, I think, to have that reaction. My parents' poetry influenced me, though, even if I spent so long denying it. It was either be against them or become like them, and I didn't see much room for compromise.

You can escape once, my mother had written in one of the poems in *The Solitary Woman*. *But if you try again, you end up where you began.*

My next few days were split between Villa Christina and *Eleni*. I avoided the main town, which felt too glitzy for me, particularly in the evenings, when its visitors would get dressed up and stroll around, preening, before settling in for dinner. I would order my food to go and eat in the pension courtyard. The woman with the pipe had left, and while I could tell other people were staying at Villa Christina by the towels they hung to dry outside their rooms, I rarely encountered them. It was for the best: I smelled. I hadn't brought enough clothes for a full week and my shirts were infused with a combination of sweat, sea water and gasoline. Even my shorts were edged in salt stains from where they'd gotten wet and then dried.

Midway through the week, however, I went to the movies. One of the open-air cinemas played classics, and the night I chose to go it was *Bonnie and Clyde*. I bought a bag of popcorn, found a seat, and then kept getting distracted by the night sky. Even with the brightness of the screen, the stars above us were visible. I watched the moon slowly creep higher. Almost full, but not quite.

I only paid attention to the movie at the end. I knew Bonnie and Clyde's ultimate fate, but I couldn't remember exactly how it happened. It wasn't during a bank robbery; instead they were set up, tricked into thinking they were helping with a flat tire and then shot dead. Right. The thing about Bonnie and Clyde is that, regardless of their doomed outcome, their partnership was exciting. A team against the world.

Anna and I had clashed over my return to Greece, even though we'd claimed to have the same goal: to stay together. We just had different visions of how to do it, and after I made the decision to leave, we lost faith in our ability to act as one. I don't think my parents ever had that kind of struggle. Maybe their problem was too much proximity, a single eye instead of separate ones.

With Larissa, I'd been reminded of the rush from being with someone despite all odds. It created a space in your life you didn't know you had, cleaved you open. Walking around Kypseli with her had made it feel new and exciting, not new and unfamiliar like it had felt when I'd first arrived, all alone. A part of me still thought I could marry her, or that we could've eloped when we'd gone to Meteora.

When the movie ended, I walked back to Villa Christina around the time Larissa would've been closing up Pet Corner. She was probably alone with the rabbits, the fish. I wanted to call her, even if it was just to thank her, but what was I thanking her for exactly?

I wondered what would happen if I told Anna about Larissa. Would she tell me about Daniel in return? Maybe that's all we needed to return to our steady state, us as a married couple. My relationship with Larissa hadn't been in retaliation against Anna for Daniel—it was a separate thing—but knowing that Anna was probably still seeing him diminished some of the guilt I felt. I was being fair, wasn't I? I'd thought about it often—fairness, balance—that what I was doing cancelled out whatever Anna had done or was still doing. But I hoped that Zoe wouldn't marry someone like me or have a relationship like ours. She deserved someone who wouldn't leave, someone who would know how to fight for her, regardless of the circumstances.

I saw Costa again a few days later when I brought the boat in for the afternoon. He helped me tie it up. The water had been choppy like when I'd first arrived, and some waves had washed up inside, soaking the food I'd left on the floor. The motor had stalled for a second and I'd worried that it might flood. *Eleni* had been my impenetrable fortress at first, but now I realized I didn't even know where the life jacket was stored.

"You're leaving tomorrow?" Costa asked.

"I might stay another day."

"You should!" he said. "You look good. You need more sun!"

It would've been nice to stay longer. The light that shone into my room in the late afternoon was a vibrant orange and pink, the perfect colour to restore any depleted energy. It was a cure for my bad-luck phase and I knew I needed a few more rounds of it. I had things to do in Athens, though.

I hadn't taken *Eleni* out in the evening yet and figured this would be my last chance to do it, to go for a sunset ride around the island and then leave in the morning.

That evening after dinner, I walked over to the harbour. People were still swimming; I could see their heads bobbing in the water. Two older women in unnecessary sun hats gossiped loudly to each other a hundred feet out as they treaded water, and the sounds of their voices carried across to shore. A horse-drawn carriage clomped behind me and rang its bell.

The sea was darker now, and the sky was greyish blue with streaks of pink. I put the key in the ignition and motored away from the dock. I kept my distance from the few boats also out on the water. I wanted to take in my surroundings in silence, as if I'd paddled out in a canoe. Anna and I had canoed once together when we'd visited Kirkland Lake, where she'd spent a few years as a child. We'd gone first thing in the morning, and the water had been glassy and still, the only sound our oars dipping into the water. I'd sat in the stern to steer, and we'd hugged the edge of the lake, uncertain of our abilities to go out any further. Uncertain, but not worried. At the time, I'd had no idea that I'd eventually embrace the water, the sea, but here I was. She was pregnant then, and we hadn't known that, either.

I regretted not bringing a camera to show Zoe what this looked like, how peaceful it was. I would tell her about it in Athens as soon as I got back. In the meantime I would fish. Costa had told me that they were easier to catch later in the day, when they would swim to the surface toward the waning sun and then, when it was dark, the moon. Fishing and drifting would be nice. I cut the engine, and listened for the silence.

ZOE

Back in the motel, our bed still hadn't been made, and everything seemed cheaper and more worn-out than when we'd checked in. Even the pink tiles in the bathroom had a stale, yellow tinge to them. The walls looked like they were made of papier-mâché, like I could smash my fist right through them, easy. Peter sat on the bed, but the room depressed me, and I suggested we try swimming. We could go in our underwear like I'd done at Mom's hotel in Montreal.

The pool was small, the water greenish, and the room smelled so overwhelmingly of chlorine that it had to have been clean. We jumped in. The man was right, the water was warm. While Peter stayed in the shallow end, I ducked under and swam to the other side. I did a few laps and then took a break in the deep end.

"You're a good swimmer," he said.

"Thanks." I floated, and my submerged ears made him sound far away.

He swam up to where I was floating. "I'm going back to the room."

"Are you okay?"

"I'm fine, I'm just not really feeling this. Don't rush, I'll see you there."

I felt like I should go back with him, but remained in the water and watched him wrap himself in a threadbare towel and leave. I closed my eyes.

It was so easy to float. At that moment, it was inconceivable that anyone could die like this, that they might sink and never come back up. You don't have to try too hard; your body fat does it for you. Even when Peter and I had fallen through a frozen lake we hadn't gotten hurt. Water doesn't have to be dangerous, I reminded myself. In fact, I usually felt safer in the water. Buoyant. Light. I dunked my head under one more time. I thought of my grandmother's poem about the Graeae:

I swam down and closed
my watery eyes,
grabbed a handful of sand from
the bottom of the sea.

I still occasionally had nightmares about my father's last moments, but in the motel pool I imagined him floating on his back like I was right then. Instead of the water-stained ceiling, he would've been looking up at the sky. He used to tell me about the quality of light in Greece, how different it was from North America. I'd seen this light, too, but couldn't figure out what was so special about it. It had been so harsh when I'd been there for his funeral. I tried to conjure a different version of the light I'd seen in Athens. If I could do it and we really did share one eye, then I'd know that what he saw was good. Something clear and warm. Maybe my father hadn't struggled or choked in the water, maybe he was just carried away, lulled to sleep by the waves and bathed in that special light, not even aware of what was happening to him.

I stayed in the pool until my fingertips were wrinkly. I padded back to our room and found Peter stretched out on the bed. I sat down next to him, and he angled himself so that his head was resting in my lap. After a few minutes he was sniffling.

"Peter?" I asked.

"I don't know what's wrong. I'm sorry," he said. He sat up and started crying, his head in his hands. When someone is sad, it's like they speak a language you don't understand. You want to communicate with them, but all you can say are easy one- and two-syllable words, nothing too complex that can truly touch the core of their sadness. When my father died, I realized that it was okay, that the simplest words could still make a difference and that even when you travel to foreign lands, people are more appreciative of your fumbled, awkward attempts than silence. Most people don't attempt, though; they're too scared.

"It's okay," I said, and rubbed his shoulder. "You don't have to apologize."

"I'm just confused about everything. I don't know what I'm doing with my life."

"Me neither."

He stopped crying.

"Maybe now's not the best time to get married." I said it first.

"Yeah," he agreed, almost too quickly. "We don't even have witnesses."

"We should've gone to Vegas. An Elvis impersonator could've married us."

"It would've been warm there, too."

"The car would've broken down, though."

"An excuse to stay."

I thought of the first time I'd had a fight with Hugo—he was leaving to see his friends, but I'd expected the two of us to spend the night together. *I just want you to think about my feelings, too*, I said. The words reflected what I wanted to say, but only approximately. I was reeling off a script I knew in my head, one I'd picked up from watching movies and reading books and eavesdropping on other couples in the street. I wondered if I'd tried following the same script with Peter, just speeding it up. I'd jumped to the part at the end, right before *happily ever after*. It wasn't that easy.

"So what are we going to do now?" Peter asked.

"I have to go back to Montreal. I have school."

"We can leave first thing in the morning."

"You don't have to drive me. I'll take the bus."

He wiped his nose. "Maybe that's a better idea."

While Peter took a shower, I got dressed, took the car keys and drove to the bus station to look at the schedule. I could've figured out a way to find it online, but I needed to be on my own for a few minutes. The marriage-licence application was on the seat beside me. Peter's handwriting slanted to the right at an even keel. This was the first time I'd really looked at it. We didn't know everything about each other, but I had a feeling that we knew more than most people.

There was so much I'd never know about anyone I loved. It was hard to accept, although sometimes, like while driving around Niagara Falls alone, I could almost do it.

I still hoped that everything I really needed to know would find its way to me eventually. Maybe I just thought this to make myself feel better about my father, but I was optimistic that, given enough time, I could piece together whatever meagre scraps I had into something larger, even for him. I'd started feeling like this in Athens when I'd had the chance to see parts of the life he lived before he died: the chair he sat in when I talked to him on the phone, the balcony he ate dinner on.

My grandmother's book was another piece, too. Whenever I translated a line, he would feel close to me. I was going slowly, but maybe it was on purpose—as long as the book remained untranslated, I'd have new information about my father to discover, even if it was indirect, oblique, and not about him at all. And the book revealed things to me anyway.

In Athens I'd met my father's neighbours, and they'd shared some stories about him that I'd never heard. The one that struck me the most was about their pet turtle. My father had taken an interest in it and bought it toys and food. I'd held the turtle in my hands and looked at its squat face. It opened its mouth and wiggled its legs, slowly. That my father, who didn't care about animals when I'd known him, had shown affection to the turtle made me feel better. I didn't think he'd been interested in it in and of itself; I knew he'd somehow connected it to me. I was the one who'd always pestered him about a pet. It was the only time on the trip that I'd been happy, watching this little turtle.

The turtle was named Bouboulina, which I would've forgotten unless I hadn't seen it in *The Solitary Woman*. My grandmother had written a poem about the person the turtle was named after, and when I'd been looking for proper nouns and found it, the story about the turtle came back to me. I still hadn't translated the poem, though; I was saving it. I would look at it on my way home.

There was a bus from Niagara Falls that left for Montreal the next morning, but there were also more frequent buses to Toronto since it was so much closer. I bought a ticket to Toronto that left later in the evening, even though I could've spent one more night with Peter. I didn't feel badly about leaving so quickly, though. Now that our plans had changed again, it didn't seem right to extend it. We'd reached the end of this phase, whatever it was. He could visit me in Montreal eventually, or we might never speak again, just e-mail. I imagined us meeting later, when we were seventy, eighty years old. Old and grey. I wished I could've asked a psychic about us, peered into a crystal ball to see how we turned out.

"I got you a present," Peter said when I got back. "Close your eyes."

I obliged and held out my hand. He gave me what felt like a plastic egg: a vending-machine prize. I popped it open and inside there was a fluorescent pink ring with a fake plastic diamond.

"I didn't plan it," Peter said. "It just came out."

"It's fate." The ring, child-sized, fit only on my pinkie. "It's so beautiful."

"It was only a dollar. A loonie."

"It's priceless."

We wanted one nice dinner before I left, but didn't know what qualified as "nice" in Niagara Falls—a hotel buffet, a chain restaurant, Denny's? We ended up at a steakhouse. Steak and baked potatoes was grown-up and formal, and, we were starving, too. After days of fast food and street vendors, I craved bloody meat. The knives they gave us to cut the steak were massive, as if we were going to eat dinosaurs, and they made us laugh so much that we hid them in my bag on the way out.

Peter drove me to the bus station. It had started raining, a cold icy rain, and I worried that his tires wouldn't be good enough for the roads. His eyelashes got all stuck together and turned dark when they were wet, like he was wearing mascara.

"Take this." He gave me the shrunken head.

I wrapped it carefully in a shirt and placed it at the top of the backpack. "What are you going to do tonight?"

"I might go to a casino."

"You should. You'll win something."

His eyes were bright with tears, but neither of us cried, and we didn't say "I love you" either.

"I'll e-mail you when I'm home," he said.

"Don't take any detours."

"Okay."

"And don't walk on any frozen lakes."

"Not without you."

We hugged and kissed, and when he left, I slipped off the ring. My souvenirs of Peter made a tiny poem:

a steak knife
a pink plastic ring
a shrunken head
a photo of us going over Niagara Falls in a barrel

I called my mother at home while I waited to board the bus. Even though she'd just returned from Paris, she answered immediately, like she'd been sitting by the phone all this time, waiting.

"Where are you now?" she asked.

"Niagara Falls, but I'm about to get on a bus to Toronto."

"By yourself? What about Emily?"

"By myself. Emily wasn't actually with me."

"Who have you been with, then?"

I could've lied again and ignored her question, but for once I could also just tell her the truth. "I'm with a guy I met on the Internet. We almost got married. We didn't. We won't."

"A guy from the Internet?"

"He's nice."

I expected her to reply with more questions, but instead she said, "Daniel proposed to me a few days ago. I didn't accept, though."

"What? Why not?"

"I think I felt guilty."

"Why?"

"Because of your father."

"Really?"

"Yes."

"You were practically divorced by the time he moved." I thought she knew I'd picked up on the cues of their weakening marriage before he moved. That my mother still considered Dad a barrier to her relationship with Daniel—Daniel who I'd known for years, Daniel who was dependable and good—surprised me.

"You thought that?"

"You were hardly talking. I asked him once, and he mentioned you had problems."

"Why did you ask him and not me?"

"I don't know."

We were both quiet for a minute.

"Are you sure you're okay?" she asked. "You're safe? You still have enough money?"

"Yes, Mom."

"When will you get here?"

"Late, around eleven. You don't have to pick me up. I'll take a cab."

I knew she would be there when the bus pulled into the station, though, and I knew that I would look for her.

The bus station in Niagara Falls looked like the one in Montreal, Albany, New York City. Brown, dirty, illuminated by tracks of fluorescent lights. Everyone looks the same, too, each of us with bags under our eyes, weighted down by backpacks and suitcases, holding paper cups of coffee. In the bathroom I studied my face, tried to see if it had changed, but I just looked worn-out and my hair was frizzy and my skin was blotchy, even though I still hadn't cried.

I got a window seat on the bus. No one sat beside me; it was only half-full. I thought about whether I would call Hugo back in Montreal, and then realized that I didn't really care either way. Sometimes I worried that people never got over anything, that I was doomed to be haunted by my father's death forever, doomed to worrying I would always be alone. Sadness and fear were occasionally diminished, but, given the right circumstances, they could flare up again as fresh and fierce as the first time I had felt those emotions. It was a relief to not feel anything for Hugo anymore, not even a twinge. And, I was happy. Or hopeful? Weren't they almost the same thing?

I remembered a some lines I'd translated from my grandmother's book:

It's Easter again and
the flowers have returned.
I knew they would come back.

A string of lights along the highway blinked yellow, sometimes blue. We passed a truck, and I stared at the driver, but he didn't notice me. I tried it again with the next truck, concentrating so hard it exhausted me, and this time the driver did look over, but I don't think he really saw me through the tinted windows. I played a game like this when I was younger where I would stare at people in other cars while we sat at red lights to test if they could feel my gaze. When they did, I would whip my head around quickly in the opposite direction, delighted and embarrassed.

I used that same level of concentration to think of Peter. I wasn't praying exactly, but I pictured him at the casino winning the jackpot. I saw him stick a quarter into a machine and leave with a million more of them, the silver coins spilling out of his pockets like shards of glass. If it happened, if he won, I knew he would offer them to me, but I also knew I wouldn't take them. I didn't need them. I was sure of that.